"HERE THEY COME!"
ARCHIE SHOUTED.

All conversation among the Black Eagles was cut off by the abrupt appearance of Pathet Lao infantrymen. Trigger fingers pumped, grenades were launched, and streams of bullets roared out of the defenders' positions. The Red riflemen stormed into the metal hell, going down in screaming shrieks like wheat falling in front of an invisible combine. Suddenly it was over. Suddenly — silence.

Lieutenant Colonel Robert Falconi's voice seemed muted and hollow as he gave his orders:

"The Soviet tanks will get here anytime. We've got to get the hell out of here."

"Where in the blazes are we going, sir?" Archie asked. "They'll catch up. Then what'll we do?"

Falconi shrugged. "You never figured on living forever, did you?"

BLACK EAGLES
by John Lansing

They're the best jungle fighters the United States has to offer. No matter where Charlie is hiding, The Eagles will find him! They're the greatest unsung heroes of the dirtiest, most challenging war of all time!

Available wherever paperbacks are sold, or order direct from the Publisher. Send cover price plus 50¢ per copy for mailing and handling to Zebra Books, Dept. 2713, 475 Park Avenue South, New York, N.Y. 10016. Residents of New York, New Jersey and Pennsylvania must include sales tax. DO NOT SEND CASH.

HOA-TIEN KILLERS #19

THE BLACK EAGLES

JOHN LANSING

ZEBRA BOOKS
KENSINGTON PUBLISHING CORP.

ZEBRA BOOKS

are published by

Kensington Publishing Corp.
475 Park Avenue South
New York, NY 10016

First printing: July 1989

Printed in the United States of America

This book is dedicated to
XVIII Airborne Corps Artillery

Special Acknowledgement
to Patrick E. Andrews

ROSTER OF THE BLACK EAGLES

COMMAND ELEMENT

Lieutenant Colonel Robert Falconi, *U.S. Army,*
Commander
Sergeant Archie Dobbs, *U.S. Army,*
Detachment Scout

ALPHA ASSAULT TEAM

First Lieutenant Ray Swift Elk, *U.S. Army,*
Team Leader
Sgt. 1st Class Calvin Culpepper, *U.S. Army,*
Senior Rifleman
(Demolitions Sergeant)
Staff Sgt. Paulo Garcia, *U.S. Marine Corps,*
Grenadier
(Intelligence Sergeant)
Sergeant Steve Matsuno, *U.S. Army,*
LAWS*
Petty Officer 3rd Class Blue Richards, *U.S. Navy,*
Rifleman
(Demolitions Specialist)

BRAVO ASSAULT TEAM

Sgt. Maj. Top Gordon, *U.S. Army*,
Team Leader
Sgt. 1st Class Malpractice McCorkel, *U.S. Army*,
Senior Rifleman
(Medical Sergeant)
Sergeant Loco Padilla, *U.S. Marine Corps*,
Grenadier
Sergeant Gunnar Olson, *U.S. Army*,
LAWS*
(Supply Sergeant)
Sergeant Ky Luyen, *South Vietnamese Army*,
Rifleman

* Light Antitank Weapon System

PROLOGUE

Chuck Fagin and Andrea Thuy stood at the edge of Camp Nui Dep's airstrip with Major Rory Riley, the commander of both the garrison and the Special Forces "B" Detachment stationed there. All three eagerly scanned the horizon, looking for any telltale sign of an approaching aircraft. Finally the Air Force sergeant in the control bunker yelled out at them. "ETA is fifteen minutes, folks."

"Are you sure it's our guys?" Fagin asked.

The sergeant shouted, "Roger! The password and countersign are proper. Those are your buddies coming in."

"It's about time," Andrea said. The beautiful Eurasian woman relaxed her vigil. "I don't know why I'm so anxious. We've already gotten the official word there has been no casualties."

"You just can't wait to see Falconi," Major Riley said.

Andrea smiled. "Perhaps you're right, Rory."

"Well, I know why I'm nervous," Fagin said.

"You should be," Rory Riley said. "Man!"

"Hey," Fagin protested. "It's my job, ain't it?"

"Yeah, but—" Riley let the words hang.

"Everybody picks on me," Fagin complained.

"It's only because you deserve it, Chuck," Andrea said.

"Don't I get credit on a few things?" Fagin asked. "I worked a paperwork miracle on the ex-Viet Cong Luyen Ky, didn't I?"

"Speaking of credit," Andrea said. "I helped out a little bit, huh?"

"Okay. Okay. You did a little," Fagin said. Then he changed his tune. "You did a *lot*."

"The guy is cleared and a sworn into the South Vietnamese Army by Major Ngubo at Camp Mot," Andrea said. "I arranged for the rather impressive ceremony. I only wish we could have been there to see it."

"But it was me that got him a sergeancy, right?"

"Right," Andrea agreed. "Remember, I saw to it that he received an immediate assignment to the Black Eagle Detachment, right?"

"Right."

"That's no big deal," Riley said. "Who else is gonna take a half-crazy ex-Viet Cong except full crazies like the Black Eagles?"

The aircraft finally came into view. It swung out for a long approach into the camp. Rory Riley pulled his binoculars from their case. He focused it on the plane. "Are them APCs still with 'em?"

"No," Fagin said shaking his head. "They left one at Camp Mot with the ARVN rangers and the other at Camp Ba with the Australians. Those guys will put 'em to good use."

The C-130 was finally visible as it closed in. The Air Force sergeant gave the transport aircraft a final clearance to land. Straightening out into a gradual descent, the big airplane dropped smoothly, until gently touching down, its tires squealing in protest when they hit the hardpacked earth of the runway.

Churning up clouds of dust, the C-130 taxied nearer, then swung around. The crew chief opened the passenger door and jumped down to the ground, installing a stepladder for the men getting off.

The Black Eagles came out one by one. An extra man, Sergeant Luyen Ky, dressed in a brand-new tiger fatigue uniform, was with them. Falconi led the way. As he approached the three people who came to greet them, he stopped. He stared at Chuck Fagin's battered old canvas briefcase the CIA officer held in his hand.

"Goddamnit, Fagin!" Falconi exclaimed. "Is there an OPLAN in there?"

"Yes," Fagin said. "Sorry about that."

Andrea leaned close to Fagin and whispered, "Are you going to tell them about the Russian tanks now or later?"

"Later," Fagin whispered back. "Much, much later. In fact, I'm gonna put off that bit of news until the absolute last minute."

The entire detachment, happy to be back but apprehensive about seeing Fagin and his infamous briefcase, left the airstrip and walked wearily down to its bunker.

The war was far from over.

CHAPTER 1

The group slowly continued their stroll from the airfield through Camp Nui Dep in the direction of the Black Eagle Detachment bunker. Major Rory Riley, the commander of the Green Berets stationed in the fortified garrison, walked beside Lieutenant Colonel Robert Falconi, the leader of the Black Eagles. The two officers had once been antagonists, but Falconi's rescue of Riley from captivity by the Viet Cong caused a big change in the major's attitude. From that moment on, Riley was determined to be pals with the lieutenant colonel.

Rory grinned. "Fagin tells me you and your guys rode through this last operation."

"Yeah," Falconi said. "We had a couple of armored personnel carriers."

"No shit?" Riley remarked. "What kind?"

"Cadillac-Gages," Falconi answered.

"Those are great fighting vehicles," Riley said. "No tracks, right?"

"Right. That made for a quieter ride at least," Falconi said.

"How'd you like 'em?" Riley asked.

"I'd rather do my fighting on foot," Falconi admitted. "Which is exactly what I did most of the time. I

13

left a driver and gunner in each vehicle while the rest of us went into the jungle after the bastards."

"That's a different armored cavalry tactic," Riley said in an approving tone. "Most of those guys wouldn't leave their APCs if the whole damned war depended on it."

"My detachment didn't like to spend long hours cooped up inside the hulls anyhow," Falconi said.

When they reached the Green Beret headquarters bunker, Riley stopped and offered his hand to Falconi. "Well, I guess the only thing I can say is 'Welcome Back'."

Falconi shook hands with his friend. "I'm just glad that we're *all* back. That's the important thing. Anyway, it's good to see you again, Rory."

"Same here, Falconi. You know where I flop. Drop on by for a couple of cold ones when you get a chance. If there's anything I can do for you, let me know, okay?"

"Sure," Falconi said. "As soon as we get whatever bad news Fagin has for us, I'll be over and we'll hoist a few. I'll fill you in on how things went this last time."

"Don't forget," Riley said. "Until later, huh?"

When Falconi resumed his walk, he was joined by Andrea Thuy and Chuck Fagin. They flanked him as the group continued its casual way back to the Black Eagle bunker. The Black Eagle commander didn't waste any time. The fact that Fagin had brought his briefcase along was a sure sign that another operation was in the wind. He decided not to wait for the CIA officer to spring any bad news on him. "Okay, Fagin, what's it going to be this time?"

"Laos," Fagin said. "But before we get into that, I've got some interesting admin poop. Two new guys have been assigned to you. Both are veteran sergeants.

One is a marine, the other out of Special Forces."

"It's about time," Falconi said with enthusiasm. "I've been wanting to build back up over since Operation Hellhound."

"With Ky, that gives us an even dozen now," Falconi said. "I think I'll reorganize the detachment back into a couple of fire teams."

Andrea interjected. "Make that *assault* teams, Robert."

"Damn!" Falconi exclaimed knowing her remark would have something to do with the next mission. "I'm not going to ask any more questions until we go over the OPLAN."

Two strangers were sitting outside the Black Eagle bunker when the detachment arrived. Everyone gathered around while Fagin made introductions. He motioned to a slim Chicano who had a shaven head and a most determined expression on his face.

"Guys," Fagin said. "This is Sergeant Roberto Padilla out of the Marine Corps."

Padilla nodded. "Hi ya," he said, carefully noting each of the Black Eagles. Then he saw Paulo Garcia. He broke into a wide grin. "Hey, Paulo! So this is where you're hanging your cover now, huh?"

"Yeah, Loco," Paulo said. "How've you been?"

"Pretty good," Padilla replied.

"Loco?" Fagin queried.

"My nickname," Padilla explained. "It means 'crazy' in Spanish."

Paulo laughed. "Now you know what kind of guy he is."

"If he got that nickname in the Corps," Fagin said, "he must really deserve it."

"He does," Paulo assured them all.

"The next guy is Sergeant Steve Matsuno out of Special Forces," Fagin said.

A short, stocky Japanese-American stood up. "Glad to meet you guys," he said. He moved with a fluid, athletic grace. He gave Falconi a direct look. "I hear you're a hell of a *karateka*, sir."

"I know a couple of moves," Falconi said.

"Maybe we can work out," Matsuno said.

Falconi nodded. "You bet."

Then the Black Eagles introduced themselves one by one. The two new men were not particularly surprised by Ky Luyen until they learned that he was not only an ex-Viet Cong, but had only recently left his former unit. In fact, he had been a prisoner of the Detachment until he defected during their last operation along a highway in the western reaches of South Vietnam.

Then Fagin took the floor again. "Okay. Before you go down into the bunker to unpack and relax, let me say that you're right if you assumed I'm bringing you another mission." He raised the well-known canvas briefcase. "You guys know when I tote this baby it always has an OPLAN in it."

"So soon?" Archie Dobbs grumbled.

"Yeah," Fagin said. "But listen up for the good news. You'll have vehicles again."

Archie was in a mood to bitch. "More goddamned APCs?"

"Not this time," Fagin said. "Jeeps—quarter-tons with recoilless rifles mounted on them. Anti-tank stuff."

Now it was Falconi who spoke. His eyes narrowed with suspicion. "Did I hear you say anti-tank as in 'going against armored forces'?"

Fagin displayed an apologetic grin. "That, Colonel Falconi, is exactly what you heard."

Steve Matsuno raised his hand. "Mister Fagin."

Fagin ignored him, continuing to speak to Falconi.

"It's not really as bad as it sounds, Falconi. You and the guys will be armed with the latest in weaponry for the mission."

"Mister Fagin!" Matsuno said again.

Fagin finally looked at him. "What?"

"There ain't gonna be any jeeps with recoilless rifles," Steve said. He pointed to three crates stacked near the bunker entrance. "That's our anti-tank stuff there."

Sergeant Major Top Gordon walked over and pulled the top off one of the wooden boxes. "There ain't nothing in here but stove pipes!"

"They're LAWS, Sergeant Major," Matsuno explained.

"What're LAWS?" Top demanded to know.

"Light Anti-tank Weapon System," Matsuno answered. "That's the official acronym for that hardware."

Top frowned. "That still don't tell me shit."

"I suppose the best way to describe them would be to say that they're disposable anti-tank rockets."

Now it was Fagin's turn to sputter. "When did this happen?" he demanded. "General Taggart promised me—"

Matsuno shrugged. "All I know is that when I got on the plane at Peterson, they put these LAWS aboard, too."

"I was supposed to get some jeeps to fly down here," Fagin said angrily.

"I don't think so, Mister Fagin," Matsuno said. "I was assigned on the basis of my experience with these babies."

"Well, Fagin," Falconi said, almost sneering. "I see you're out of step again." Knowing there was nothing to gain by complaining about the situation, the Black Eagle commander turned his full attention to the

17

Japanese-American. "Since you're an expert, tell me your opinion of those disposable rockets in combat."

"Sorry, sir," Matsuno said. "To my best knowledge, they've never been used in actual battle."

Now Falconi glared at Fagin. "What the hell does the OPLAN say about our anti-tank weaponry?"

"How the hell should I know?" Fagin said angrily. "You know I'm not allowed to look at the goddamned paperwork until I get out here. There's even a seal on it."

Andrea, who worked as Fagin's administrative assistant, intervened in the situation that threatened to become explosive. "Nobody told us anything except that there were supposed to be jeeps, Robert," she said.

Falconi pointed at Fagin. "He still should have—"

Now Andrea became angry. Her eyes seemed to flash sparks as she spoke. "I'm tired of you picking on Chuck all the time! He does plenty for you and your guys. Yet, you continually heap shit all over him."

Now it was Fagin's turn to be the peacemaker. "Hold it! Things are getting too hot. Let's all relax now. We've got a job to do."

Falconi nodded. "Okay. But one of these days, Fagin, I want to go over your head and talk to the sons of bitches who plan these operations."

Fagin shook his head. "No way."

"We'll talk about it later," Falconi said. While all the talking was going on, he'd mentally broken his detachment down into two combat teams. "All right! Listen up!" he said sharply.

When Falconi used that tone of voice, the men knew that something damned important was either about to be said or done. They gave their full attention to the commanding officer.

"Archie is back to being scout and will be with me,"

18

Falconi announced. "Alpha Team will be run by Ray Swift Elk. Calvin, Paulo, and Blue are Alphas. And so are—" He pointed to Sergeant Steve Matsuno. "—you."

"Yes, sir," Matsuno said. He walked over to where the other men had gathered around the Sioux Indian officer.

"The rest of you," Falconi said, "Malpractice, Gunnar, Ky, and Padilla are Bravos under the sergeant major."

"Gather 'round me, boys," Top Gordon said.

"I want to see a lot of team integrity," Falconi said. "That means you'll do everything together. When I dismiss you, I want the Alphas to take the bunks on the left side of the bunker, and the Bravos on the right. Archie can use any convenient spot he wants. Any questions?" He paused. "Okay. Follow me on down into the bunker."

As the commander led his men into their billets, Andrea Thuy grabbed Chuck Fagin's arm and pulled him to the side. "I want to talk to you!"

"You sound mad," Fagin said.

"I am," Andrea said. "Why don't you defend yourself when those guys get on your case? You knew that the substitution of those LAWS for the jeeps had nothing to do with you."

"So what?" Fagin said with a grin and a shrug.

"So what? They're holding you responsible for a foul up that you had nothing to do with," Andrea said.

"Let me explain this to you," Fagin said. "Those guys get a royal screwing on every mission that they go out on."

"I know that, Andrea said. "I've been out with them three or four times myself, remember?"

"Okay. And those screw ups can be caused by just

19

about anybody," Fagin went on. "For example, who didn't deliver those jeeps for this mission? General Taggart? Maybe. Or was it a G4 who decided to send the damned things somewhere else? Maybe. Or was it a stupid goddamned clerk who put the paperwork in the wrong cubbyhole? Maybe."

"I don't understand what you're getting at," Andrea said.

"The Black Eagles can't get at those people who really cause them grief," Fagin explained. "Their rage at the incompetent sonofabitches would be empty emotion. But they can get mad at me—*me!* And they've got somebody they can see and cuss out and yell at and dump their anger on."

Now Andrea understood. "You must like playing the thankless role of a safety valve, Chuck."

"Yeah. It's good for their morale, Andrea," Fagin said. "And it's no skin off my ass."

"But they should know of the countless times you've gone out on a limb for them," Andrea said. "Robert Falconi should be told of how you've yelled and hollered at your own superiors to straighten things out when you could."

Fagin shook his head. "No way. And I want you to promise me that you'll never tell them the truth as long as the Black Eagles are in action in this war."

"Chuck—"

He held up his hand. "After we're out of Southeast Asia, you can blab away to your heart's content. But in the meantime, don't say anything. Promise?"

Andrea hesitated, but finally nodded her head. "Okay. I promise. But I think you're a—" She paused again, then broke into a big smile. "I think you're a hell of a fine man, Chuck Fagin."

"Aw!" he said, feigning shyness and modesty. "You're only saying that 'cause it's true." He gestured at the bunker entrance. "C'mon. Let's get down there and get this mission on the road.

"Yes, sir!"

They went down the steps into the interior of the Black Eagles quarters. When Chuck entered, there was a chorus of catcalls, hisses, and boos.

"Thank you, gentlemen," the CIA officer said. "I love you, too!"

CHAPTER 2

While the men arranged themselves and their gear in the bunker's large room, Lieutenant Colonel Robert Falconi, Lieutenant Ray Swift Elk, and Sergeant Major Top Gordon went off with Chuck Fagin and Andrea Thuy into the colonel's small office.

Once inside, they all sat down around the table there. Chuck Fagin opened his famous briefcase and removed a heavy manila envelope. "Please note the seal is intact," he said. "I don't want anybody to think I've been peeking."

Then, without waiting for any sort of reply, he broke the wax device. Withdrawing several documents from the package, he passed one to each of the others.

"This is the OPLAN for Operation Hoa-Tien," Fagin said. "I suggest a quick but careful reading." He sat down to review his own copy of the war plans. "I noticed there was also a packet of maps to go with the stuff. But right now I think the OPLAN will be enough to keep our minds occupied."

"Then let's knock off the bullshit," Falconi said irritably. "We've got some damned important information to suck in and damned little time to do it."

This OPLAN—Operations Plan—was the primary

document for the operation planing. The task for the Black Eagles would be to take that document and rewrite it to fit specifics. Once it was altered and accepted, it became an OPORD—Operations Order—which would be their bible for the coming mission.

Falconi perused the OPLAN carefully, noting each detail. "A hell of a note," he complained. "The assholes in G3 knew we wouldn't have those jeeps quite a while ago. They're not even mentioned here."

Top Gordon had misgivings. "I don't know about those LAWS, sir. Even that new guy Matsuno has never used them in combat. What if they don't perform up to standards?"

"Then, Sergeant Major, we're all going to be very, very dead," Falconi said. He laid his copy of the OPLAN down. "But let's not dwell on that. Get the extra copies and pass them out among the men."

"Yes, sir," Top said, gathering up nine OPLANS.

"I'll leave it up to you to assign the areas of responsibilities," Falconi said. "We should be able to have the briefing in twenty-four hours. This stuff is pretty cut and dried."

"Yes, sir," Top said. He went outside into the large billeting area. "At ease!" he hollered.

The men, who had been talking among themselves, quickly shut up.

"Ever'body gets a copy," Top said. "You know what they are and you know what you gotta do with 'em." As he passed them out, he assigned particular jobs. "Paulo, you've got the intelligence portion of the briefing."

"Yes, Sergeant Major," Paulo replied, taking his OPLAN.

"You'll handle the orientation on the LAWS, Matsuno," Top instructed. "You're the only guy that knows anything about those contraptions."

Matsuno nodded.

"The medical stuff is yours, Malpractice," Top said going to the detachment medic. "And Gunnar, you've got supply."

"Again?" Gunnar asked with a frown.

"Yes, again," Top said firmly.

"What about commo?" Blue Richards asked.

"Lieutenant Swift Elk is handling that," Top answered. "Calvin, you and Blue help Matsuno out on the LAWS. Padilla can work with Paulo. At this point I think it's a good idea for Ky to be Gunnar's assistant."

"What about me?" Archie asked, raising his hand.

"You'll cover terrain since you'll be the scout," Top said. "I brought a map for you." He gazed at the group. "Now ever'body's got something to do. So, goddamnit! *Do it!*"

The Black Eagles immediately went to work.

Typewriters clacked and several conferences were organized, conducted, and dismissed as that particular day dragged on into the evening.

Fagin, staying in Falconi's office, kept himself available for consultation and to answer questions as the frantic process of taking all the information and instructions in the OPLAN, then breaking it down into readable, understandable segments continued for long hours.

The Black Eagles needed no supervision for the task. Each man performed his job diligently and completely. In preparing the paperwork necessary to take a unit into battle, every paragraph, sentence, and word was important. Any omissions or sloppy reference work could leave vital questions unanswered. Ignorance was certainly not bliss when going into a combat mission that required split-second timing and decisions that had to be right.

It was a death sentence.

Paulo Garcia and Loco Padilla poured over maps, intelligence documents, reports derived from the interrogations of POWs, and Orders of Battle as they pieced together the picture of the enemy they would soon be facing.

Steve Matsuno organized his class with Calvin Culpepper and Blue Richards as he wrote down his lesson plan on the Light Anti-tank Weapons System he had to teach to the Black Eagles.

Gunnar Olson and his sidekick, ex-Viet Cong Ky Luyen, ran their butts off filling out requisitions and fetching items such as rations, ammunition, parachutes, personal gear, and equipment to replace the lost and worn stuff in the detachment. Then the overworked duo did it all again as new requirements popped up in the midst of all the hullabaloo.

Lieutenant Ray Swift Elk, besides having to look after the Alpha Assault Team, checked out the radios and wrote up signal instructions for the operation. While he was going through that song and dance, Sergeant Major Top Gordon looked after the Bravos and conferred with Lieutenant Colonel Robert Falconi on the actual concept and execution of the mission.

Malpractice McCorkel frantically made up individual medical kits for everyone while putting together a larger more complicated one that he would use in the case of seriously wounded Black Eagles. He also had sanitation to worry about, making sure everyone's shot records were up-to-date, that there were water purification tablets, salt tablets, and even fungus medicine available.

In the middle of this organized confusion, Andrea Thùy made herself useful in many ways. She typed, made coffee, answered questions, cleaned weapons, and performed dozens of other necessary chores. Although a thoroughly tested and proven combat veteran in her own right, she didn't mind the "steppin' and fetchin'" if it helped things run a bit smoother.

Nightfall came and still the work went on. Finally, one by one, the Black Eagles gathered up the final preparations of their paperwork, and took them in for Falconi's inspection. As he approved their efforts, the activity gradually died down.

Then, in the wee hours of the morning, it was quiet and peaceful as everyone was able to get into their bunk. The placid atmosphere was broken only by an occasional snort or snore from some sleeping Black Eagle.

"Drop your cocks and grab your socks!"

Sergeant Major Top Gordon's voice exploded over the sleeping men with all the subtlety of an incoming 105-millimeter artillery shell. It was nearing time for the briefing.

"I'm gonna give you a half hour to dress, wash, and eat," Top said. "Then I want you ornery bastards to set your scaly asses down on the benches in here to get this program off the ground. Go to it!"

The men, after slipping into fresh fatigue uniforms, quickly shaved. They consumed some C-ration fruit and crackers for breakfast, washing it down with canteen cupfuls of G.I. instant coffee. Top, true to his word, rounded up the Detachment and had them sitting down to begin the briefing at exactly thirty minutes after his shouted announcement.

The men, holding their individual portions of the

26

newly created OPORD, had barely settled down before Top's voice again detonated:

"Tinch-*HUT!*"

Everyone snapped to attention as Falconi led Swift Elk, Fagin, and Andrea into the room.

"Sir," Top reported with a salute. "The Detachment is all present and accounted for."

"Thank you, Sergeant Major," Falconi said. He turned to the men. "At ease. Take your seats. As Blue Richards and his colleagues in the navy would say, 'The smoking lamp is lit'." He waited for everyone to make themselves comfortable. "Okay. The mission assigned us is to infiltrate the Cammon Plateau area of Laos and destroy a North Vietnamese armored unit operating there in conjunction with Pathet Lao infantry."

Now the men understood the basic task that had been assigned to them.

Falconi continued, "Anti-communist forces in that area have been rendered useless by this mechanized aggression, leaving that gateway to the south wide open for enemy troops and supplies to pour through at their leisure."

Calvin Culpepper shook his head. "It's the same old story. We're gonna be the stoppers in a boiling bottle."

"That's it, Calvin," Falconi said. "And if we're not careful, we're going to get scalded."

"What's the general situation in the operational area, sir?" Loco Padilla asked.

"It is rapidly deteriorating," Falconi answered. "Things are so bad that operations in South Vietnam are threatened. Unless immediate and decisive action is launched, we face a real possibility of getting our butts kicked in the west."

Chuck Fagin, leaning against the wall off to the

27

side, added his own commentary. "You guys just finished opening the highway west of Ban me Thuot on your last mission. If you fall short here, those enemy tanks are going to streak through there like shit through a goose."

"Right," Falconi agreed. "There are no American troops available for deployment into Laos. The local commanders there don't have the technical expertise necessary to fight back against armored attacks. So the whole burden rests on our broad and brawny shoulders. Now if there are no questions on the mission assignment, I'll turn the program over to Paulo Garcia for the intelligence portion of the briefing."

Paulo replaced the colonel at the front of the room. "As mentioned by the colonel, we'll be going up against Pathet Lao infantry supported by North Vietnamese-manned Soviet tanks. We all know the reputation of the Pathet Lao, right?"

"Right," Archie Dobbs said. "Crazy sonofabitches that don't mind dying."

"Then you shouldn't mind killing them," Paulo said. "They are fanatic zealots who'll jazz themselves up with narcotics before going into combat. Expect massed attacks without finesse. Their commanders believe in crushing the opposition through the sheer weight of numbers."

"Lots of full-automatic firing, right?" Gunnar Olson said.

"Right," Paulo replied. "And Loco and me as grenadiers are gonna be kept busy pumping grenades through them M203 launchers. They'll outnumber the shit out of us, guys. The only way we'll be able to keep 'em off our asses is with firepower—I say again—fire*power!*"

"Tell us about the tanks, Paulo," Malpractice said.

"This ain't gonna cheer you up neither," Paulo said. "We'll be facing Soviet T-55 tanks. And there's every indication that Soviet advisors are either nearby or actually taking part in the enemy operations. Those Russki battle wagons have armor 8 inches thick and can move at 55 kilometers an hour over level ground—and that goddamned Cammon Plateau is level."

"Lovely!" Steve Matsuno said.

"That's the bad news," Paulo said. "The worst news is that they're armed with a 100-millimeter cannon and two machine guns. One is a heavy 12.7 millimeter job and its little brother is 7.62-millimeters."

"How's that armored unit put together?" Blue Richards asked.

"There're four tanks in a platoon, making sixteen in a company," Paulo answered. "Since we're going up against a battalion, you can expect no less than sixty-four of 'em coming at us."

"Holy shit!" Archie yelled. He looked at Steve Matsuno. "I hope you brought a lot of them LAWS along with you, pal."

"I didn't bring sixty-four," Matsuno said in a worried tone.

"Okay," Paulo said. "Now you know what we're going up against. I'll let Gunnar Olson give you the poop on supply."

Gunnar took the floor. "Let me get into them LAWS first off the bat. We ain't got sixty-four. All we got right now is thirty. That's about half the number we need. But we're gonna have two automatic resupply drops that'll deliver us thirty each trip. That'll make a total of ninety. Ever'body, with the exception of the colonel, the teams leaders, the grenadiers, and the scout are gonna tote five LAWS each. As the two LAWS guys use 'em up—that's me and Steve Mat-

29

suno—we'll grab a few off you guys that're carrying them."

"Hey!" Malpractice said. "How much do them god-damned things weigh?"

"Just about five pounds," Gunnar said. "That means twenty-five extra pounds along with your regular gear."

"What about other stuff we'll take in with us?" Loco Padilla asked.

"It'll be a basic issue of ammo and rations," Gunnar said. "Those will also be replenished on the two resupply drops. Ever'body understand? Good. Now I'll turn the meeting over to Archie Dobbs for the rundown on the terrain we'll be operating on."

Archie Dobbs didn't mince words. "The fucking place is flat," he said bluntly. "There's damn little natural cover and anybody taking on tanks is gonna be standing out like a payday whore in church." He unfolded a copy of the operational area map. "Look. No contour lines, no vegetation green, and only a few narrow creeks. I had a midnight consultation with Colonel Falconi and we decided that I'll keep us as close to them little waterways as possible. They're sort of natural trenches, and if some of 'em are deep enough they'll give us some protection—not from tank cannons—but at least we can hide from the bastards there. That's it, guys."

Archie returned to his seat and sat down. Sergeant First Class Malpractice McCorkel took his place to give the medical briefing. "I've prepared individual kits for ever'body. They'll include the usual first aid items as well as water purification tablets, salt tablets, and special goodies. I've put in stuff to keep you awake when you can't sleep, make you sleep when you can't doze off, make you shit, make you stop shitting, pep you up, and—" He held up a specially sealed vial. "These babies make you sleep, too. But you'll never wake up. I strongly advise their use in the event that capture by the Pathet Lao is imminent."

The solemn expressions on the men's faces showed they took their medical sergeant seriously.

"Okay," Malpractice continued. "I'll have my field surgical kit for serious wounds or illnesses. We won't be able to have a medevac when we need it, but we can make arrangements during the resupply drops that Gunnar told you about. That's the latest word on the medical front. Lieutenant Swift Elk will give you the commo report."

Ray Swift Elk, the second-in-command of the Black Eagles, was a full-blooded Oglala Sioux Indian from South Dakota. He walked with the easy grace of a born warrior as he went to the front of the room. "The reason that medevac will depend on resupply drops is that will be the only time when we will be in range for radio contact with somebody from the outside."

"What kind of radios are we gonna have, sir?" Calvin Culpepper asked.

"Our old reliables—the Prick-Sixes," Ray said. "There won't be anything with enough range to reach back to the rear bases." He made sure everyone understood the communications situation. "You all realize that means we can't yell for help just anytime we want to, right?"

There was a solemn nodding of heads.

"Okay. The old man's call sign will be 'Falcon'. Archie Dobbs will be 'Scout', and the team leaders can be raised by their unit names: Alpha and Bravo. That's it. Now the Sergeant Major will cover the execution phase of the briefing."

Now the men really perked up. Top Gordon was

going to let them know the precise times and the exact events that would take them into the mission.

"The first thing after this briefing," Top announced, "will be a class on the LAWS—Light Anti-Tank Weapon System—by Sergeant Matsuno. His assistants in this instruction will be Sergeants Culpepper and Olson." The senior non-commissioned officer paused long enough to light a cigar. "Okay. The shit goes down beginning at 1200 hours. At that time we will form up outside this bunker with bag and baggage to march down to the airfield. Once down there, we'll meet the C-130 aircraft that will fly us into the operational area for the parachute infiltration."

Archie Dobbs raised his hand. "What kinda 'chutes we got, Sergeant Major?"

"B-12 mains and T7A reserves," Top answered. "So you can see we'll be freefalling in. After chuting up and getting checked we'll meet station time aboard the aircraft at 1300 hours. Take off is 1315 and we should be over the drop zone at 1400." He tacked a large map on the wall. "There it is, gentlemen, on the south end of the operational area. Once down, we bury all chutes, then move out to look for Russian tanks."

Malpractice had a question. "Why don't we make a night infiltration? Wouldn't it be better?"

"Too dangerous on a drop zone that's been picked from a map reconnaissance," Top said. "You've got to be able to physically see where you're going to land. We chose 1400 hours because that's the siesta time for the Pathet Lao and their North Vietnamese buddies manning those tanks."

"What about them fucking Russians that are supposed to be there?" Archie asked.

"They'll be looking for you, Wiseguy," Top said. "The first Russki that brings in Archie Dobbs gets a free year's supply of borscht and all the vodka he can wash it down with."

Blue laughed. "Archie ain't worth it."

The one man who had remained silent during the entire briefing, finally spoke. The ex-Viet Cong Ky Luyen raised his hand. "What time do we fight the tanks?"

"Whenever we find 'em," Top answered. "God only knows how this thing is going to go down. If the bastards are all together, we're going to have one hell of a big battle right off the bat. If they're scattered around, we'll hit 'em piecemeal and hope Lady Luck smiles on us." The sergeant major took a drag off his cigar. "It's simple, guys, but deadly. Stay on your toes. Any more questions?"

"How long is this thing gonna last?" Blue Richards asked.

"It depends on how long it takes us to knock out sixty-four Russian T-55 tanks," Top replied. "Now let's get outside to that class. If we don't at least get some preliminary instruction on the LAWS, we'll be out there 'til doomsday."

"Yeah," Archie Dobbs said, leading the group toward the door. "Our doomsday."

CHAPTER 3

The Black Eagles, with Chuck Fagin and Andrea Thuy following, filed up the steps of the bunker and stepped outside into the hot tropical sunshine. Andrea, with something definitely on her mind, hurried through the group until she reached Calvin Culpepper. Calvin, surprised, looked at her. "Hey, Andrea. What's shaking?"

"Something very important," she answered, tugging at his arm. She led him off to the side.

The black sergeant was curious. "You look like there's something serious going down. What's on your mind?"

"Uzuri Mwanamke," Andrea said. *"That's* what's on my mind."

Calvin laughed. "How did you hear about her? Did one of the guys tell you?" Uzuri was the beautiful Ugandan woman Calvin had met during the last Black Eagle mission. He'd really gone for the African woman, but as a pacifist, she'd rebuffed him when she found out he was in a special kill-or-be-killed outfit.

"She called me hoping I could help put her in contact with you," Andrea said. "She's still working at that UNESCO orphanage in the western part of

34

Vietnam." Andrea gave Calvin a meaningful look. "Uzuri came to Saigon to see me. She's even staying at my apartment during her visit. The woman is crazy about you, Calvin."

"Hey!" Calvin said in gentle protest. "The woman bad-mouthed me, didn't she? She told me I was a damn cold-blooded killer and that all my Black Eagle buddies was gangsters."

"Yes," Andrea said. "She regrets that knee-jerk reaction to you. Uzuri changed her mind when you guys rescued her and her friends when they were held hostages on that bus by the Viet Cong. I suppose she realized there are folks in this world that don't understand anything but brute force."

"So what?" Calvin asked.

"Her change in attitude sort of puts you two more in tune with each other, doesn't it?" Andrea asked.

"We got nothing in common except we're both black," Calvin said. "And that ain't enough to bring us together. I don't care what she said to you. The bottom line is that she's a peacenik and I don't believe in turning my cheek to nobody."

"You must admit the experience of being made a prisoner by a group of people supposedly fighting for their independence probably shook her up at least a little bit," Andrea said. She reached in her pocket and brought out an envelope. "This letter is from Uzuri, Calvin. I invited her to come to my apartment. We've become friends and she's a wonderful person, really."

"She may be the most fantastic person in the world," Calvin said. "What's that got to do with me?"

"I think she's in love with you, Calvin," Andrea said.

"Oh, man! Now that's all that I need, ain't it?" Calvin said. "Here I am running all over Southeast Asia getting shot at and shooting back, and here's some woman that wants me to settle down."

Andrea gave him an inquisitive look. "If you don't really care much about her, why are you so upset by her obvious interest in you?"

"Andrea," Calvin said. "You got a way about you that really digs deep. Cool it, huh?"

"Take the letter and write her back," Andrea urged him.

"I'll take the letter, but I ain't guaranteeing I'll write back," Calvin said. He noticed the men had gotten far ahead. "I got to hurry along, Andrea. It's important that I learn about that damned LAWS thing. I don't want any Russki tanks rolling over me."

Giving Andrea a wave, he double-timed until he caught up with the group. They finally stopped at the barbed-wire perimeter of the camp.

Sergeant Steve Matsuno motioned Gunnar Olson to join him. Matsuno had one of the tubular weapons slung over his shoulder. "Okay, you guys," he said. "Gather 'round and take a seat." He waited for everyone to settle down in the dirt. Taking the weapon off his shoulder, he held it up so everyone could see it. "This," he announced, "is a 66-millimeter, lightweight, shoulder-fired, rocket launcher complete with a high-explosive anti-tank rocket. It is called a LAWS, as you've already been told."

Malpractice raised his hand. "Is it only for anti-tank use?"

Matsuno shook his head. "Nope. You could use 'em pretty effectively against bunkers and pillboxes or any other kind of structure."

"How do you load it?" Paulo Garcia asked.

"It's already loaded when you get it," Matsuno replied. "In fact the rocket is packaged inside its own launcher. But one thing I want to caution you about is the backblast. This baby is designated as an open-chambered weapon. There's no recoil, but all the propellant gases escape out the rear. That shit is dangerous to man and beast 40 meters to the rear. That means when it's tank fighting time, the assault teams will be formed in skirmish lines."

"Okay," Sergeant Major Top Gordon said impatiently. "Let's get on with shooting the goddamned thing."

Matsuno talked Gunnar through the firing procedure. The Black Eagle got into the prone position, aiming the weapon out at an imaginary target beyond the camp's barbed wire perimeter.

"Now," Matsuno said. "The best place to hit a tank is from the side or rear. The front of them big mothers has the heaviest armor. And aim toward the center."

"What's the range?" Loco Padilla asked. "I want to know how close to let one of them mothers get before I blast it."

Paulo Garcia laughed. "Loco likes to look straight into a man's eyes before he kills him."

"The maximum effective range is 200 meters," Matsuno said. "But the absolute max is 1,000 meters. Now, if there are no more questions, I'll take Gunnar through the entire firing procedures. Just make sure you guys stay off to the side there and avoid the backblast."

Gunnar dutifully obeyed Matsuno's instructions, finally pushing the trigger boot. The small weapon exploded, belching gases to the back that kicked up a cloud of swirling dust. At the same time, the rocket zipped out the front, hitting a portia tree on the edge of the jungle. It exploded, shattering the trunk into bits.

"That, gentlemen, was the exact round we'll be using in combat," Matsuno said. "The 66-millimeter

HEAT—High Explosive Anti-Tank—rocket."

Now the detachment commander spoke up. "I noticed the backblast kicked up a telltale cloud of dust and dirt. Keep that in mind, guys. That flying debris is going to give you away. We'll have to be mobile."

"—and fast!" Archie Dobbs added.

Calvin Culpepper stood up. "What's gonna be our basic tactics with them babies, sir?"

"Simple and direct," Falconi answered. "The creeks in the area are natural tank traps, if they're deep enough, and will also provide us cover. We'll do our tank killing from there when we can. But if you find yourself between that proverbial rock and hard place, you'll kick off a rocket no matter where you are."

"Will we each get a chance to fire?" Blue Richards asked.

"Sorry," Falconi said. "We don't have enough to spare at this time. I'm afraid if something happens to Matsuno or Gunnar, you'll have to learn the hard way."

Steve Matsuno grabbed the expended launcher from Gunnar and tossed it out over the barbed wire. "Like I said. This is a disposable weapon. It's not worth a damn once it's fired." He looked around the group. "Does anyone have any questions? Sound off if you do. In a situation like this, there's no such thing as a stupid one."

Everyone nodded their understanding of the simple weapon.

The sergeant major checked his watch. "It's only a half hour to station time. Get back to the bunker and grab your gear, we've got to get this mission rolling."

The Detachment quickly obeyed the senior noncommissioned officer's orders. When they got back to the bunker, they all went inside and quickly reappeared with their rucksacks and weapons. The last man was Calvin Culpepper. He walked over and handed a quickly scribbled note to Andrea.

"You said you was gonna see Uzuri, right?" he asked.

"She's at my apartment now," Andrea answered.

"Give her this, okay?" He handed the paper over.

"Sure," Andrea said smiling. "And I'll tell her that you'll see her when you get back. Right?"

Calvin shrugged. "What the hell? Okay. Tell her. I think it might do us both good to sit down and have one of them heart-to-heart chats."

Andrea smiled. "That's fine, Calvin. I think you'll both feel better."

Calvin winked. "You don't know what I wrote down in that letter."

"I know you wouldn't write anything mean or stupid," Andrea said.

"I just told her I hoped things was going fine for her," Calvin said. He hugged Andrea. "I got to go, lady. Duty calls. Goodby."

"Goodby, Calvin," Andrea said. "God bless you."

Chuck Fagin joined her. "What are you doing? Playing matchmaker?"

Andrea nodded. "For two very nice people who deserve each other." She sighed. "I wish we could go to the airstrip to say goodby."

Fagin shook his head. "Nope. Our job is done. Security regulations say that once your part of an operation is accomplished, you have to step aside. The less you know, the better off for everyone."

"Okay, Chuck," Andrea said. "Let's go down into the bunker and relax."

"Sure, kid. You want some coffee?"

"Hell, no!" Andrea exclaimed. "I need a stiff slug of that Irish whiskey of yours!"

When the Black Eagles arrived at the airstrip they found their transport—a C-130 aircraft—waiting for them. Their parachutes were neatly stacked in two rows at the edge of the runway.

"What're you waiting for?" Top bellowed. "Chute up!"

The men immediately broke down into two-man groups. The first man struggled into the harnesses while his companion helped him get properly strapped in. This included the main parachute, reserve parachute, and oxygen tank with mask. Once that was accomplished, the first Black Eagle had to get his rucksack and extra LAWS rockets hooked behind him just below the backpack of the main.

Then the second man went through the routine until finally both donned their jump helmets and were ready to form up for a jumpmaster inspection by Sergeant Major Top Gordon.

The senior NCO's checking procedure started at the top. After making sure the headgear was properly settled on with chinstrap in place, he worked his way down to the reserve parachute, paying particular attention to the ripcord and the rigger seal there. A check of the leg straps completed the front. Then the jumper turned around to have the main parachute inspected and, lastly, the equipment he had hooked onto the rigging.

Finally, with five minutes to spare, the last man was given his inspection. Even though that was Lieutenant Colonel Robert Falconi, Top showed no respect for rank or position. He went over the commander's gear with the same meticulous care he'd shown the lower rankers.

"Okay, sir," Top said gruffly. "You're strapped in there pretty good. With some luck you might make it alright."

Falconi grinned at the sergeant major's grim humor. "Now I'm full of hope."

Top winked at him and turned to the men. "In reverse stick order! Board the aircraft!"

The Black Eagles walked up the lowered ramp in the opposite order they would be jumping. Formed into two sticks, they filed to their respective seats along the side of the fuselage. The Air Force crew chief stood in the center of the aircraft interior, giving silent greetings to the parachutists. He had flown with them before and was an old friend.

Falconi and Top, the stick leaders, were the last aboard. They, like the others, struggled into the web seats. It was a difficult task with the equipment strapped to the backs of their legs.

As soon as they managed to settle down, the engines cranked over. The hydraulic lifts went to work pulling the big ramp closed. Within moments it was dark inside, the only light coming in through the portholes along the bulkheads. As the engines revved, the airplane shook, then began to roll, shaking slightly as the pilot turned it to face down the airstrip. Then the plane made its bid to get airborne. The crew chief gave the Black Eagles a "thumbs up" signal, then hurried up front to the cockpit.

Finally, with the engines' RPM going full blast, the big aircraft picked up enough speed to gently lift off the ground. Its altitude steepened as the rate of climb increased. The minutes passed slowly for the Black Eagles, the temperature dropping perceptively as the C-130 lumbered higher and higher into the Asian sky.

The air force crew chief made another quick appearance. It was to let the Black Eagle parachutists know it was time to don their oxygen masks. No time was wasted in the procedure. Any slowness could

41

easily result in oxygen starvation where physical and mental abilities would be severely curtailed. It would be deadly in the performance of a HALO jump.

After the flight was forty minutes old, the ramp was again lowered. The sight outside the aircraft was nothing but dense clouds. Falconi signaled for the men to stand up. When all were up and ready, he motioned them forward toward him. Up on the bulkhead the red alert light came on.

The jump would be made under the CARP system — Calculated Air Release Point — in which the navigator chose the time and place to tell the Detachment when to exit the aircraft. In this particular case, the officer was an experienced parachutist in his own right. He was emotionally involved in the task of getting the Black Eagles onto the correct patch of earth. When he was certain of his calculations, he pressed the green button.

Falconi and Top ran out the back of the airplane with the men crowding behind them. All quickly stabilized, assuming steady face-down positions as they plummeted to earth.

The Black Eagles could see the flat terrain thousands of feet below them. At that particular time they referred to it as the Cammon Plateau. But before the operation was over, they would have a new name for it.

The Detachment would call it hell.

CHAPTER 4

A few hours after the Black Eagles had hurled themselves into empty space above Laos, Chuck Fagin and Andrea Thuy arrived back at Peterson Field in Saigon. As they walked from the Chinook helicopter that had brought them on the return trip from Camp Nui Dep, Andrea put a restraining hand on Chuck's arm, speaking urgently:

"Cool it!" she urged him.

"Like hell I will!" he exclaimed. "I'm going to have a showdown with that sonofabitch Taggart once and for all."

"Maybe it wasn't his fault," Andrea suggested.

Fagin stopped and glared at her. "How can you say that? He was the one who assured me—*assured me*— that jeep-mounted recoilless rifles would be available for the Black Eagles on this operation."

"That still doesn't mean—"

Fagin turned away and resumed his rapid walk.

Andrea hurried after him. She was clearly worried about the results of any encounter between Fagin and the general. "Do you want me to go with you?"

"No!"

"I think I had better," she said.

"I said no," Fagin insisted.

"Then I'll wait for you back at the office," Andrea said.

"There's nothing you can do, so you better get your pretty little ass back to your apartment," Fagin said. "You've got a guest there, don't you?"

"Yes," Andrea said. "The Ugandan woman Uzuri is staying with me. I have a note for her from Calvin."

"Then you have a good reason to go home," Fagin said. "She's probably anxious to see what Sergeant Culpepper has to say to her."

Andrea tried to force some humor into the situation. "Maybe I should go to your place and start packing your things. You'll either be getting fired or heading to jail for shooting Brigadier General James Taggart."

"Go away, Andrea," Fagin said ignoring the bantering. "I'll see you tomorrow at work." He stepped up the pace, leaving her behind. When he arrived at the gate leading into the compound where the Special Operations Group headquarters building was located, he quickly flashed his ID at the MP guard. Striding across the yard, he reached the entrance and impatiently went through the ritual of being admitted to the building.

Fagin's temper flared at the military policeman's slowness in checking the admittance roster. "Can't you read any faster than that? You know who I am, goddamnit!"

"Jeez, Mister Fagin!" the MP said. "Give me a break, huh? You know the procedure. I gotta look up your name."

"Awright! Awright! Just move along will you?"

"Sure, Mister Fagin," the soldier said. "Now what's your destination in the building?"

"I'm gonna call on Taggart," Fagin answered.

"General Taggart?"

44

"Hell, yes, General Taggart! Is there another god-damned Taggart in there?"

"Just a minute, I'll look on the roster and see," the military policeman said.

"That was a goddamned rhetorical question!" Fagin almost yelled.

"Is that the same as an official inquiry?"

"No! No! Hell, no!" Fagin shouted. "It means you don't have to answer the goddamned question or take any action or nothing! Just let me in the goddamned building!"

"Well, you check out okay," the MP said. "Go ahead."

"About time!"

"Have a nice day, Mister Fagin," the guard said.

Fagin only grumbled as he went through the door. He took an elevator up to the third floor. Stepping out, he went through another painstaking scrutiny before being allowed to proceed down the hall to the office of Brigadier General James Taggart. He barged into the outer office and confronted a burly master sergeant sitting at the reception desk.

"I want to see Taggart, Blanchard," Fagin said.

Master Sergeant Tom Blanchard shook his head. "The general is busy, Fagin."

Fagin slammed his fist down on the desk. "You get on that fucking intercom and tell the sonofabitch that Fagin is out here to see him."

Blanchard stood up. "Don't bang on my desk like that, Fagin, or I'll do the same to your head."

"Yeah?" Fagin, leaning on the desk, clasped both hands together and brought them straight up in a lightning quick movement that drove them under Blanchard's chin.

The sergeant staggered back and hit the wall. But he was far from stunned. He reacted quickly, charg-

45

ing forward and diving over the desk. He collided with Fagin, making both men crash to the floor. They rolled and punched and cussed and yelled until the inner office door crashed open.

"What the fuck's going on out here!"

Brigadier General James Taggart stood there with his hands planted on his hips. He glared down at the combatants who had ceased their struggling.

Blanchard exhibited a weak smile. "Fagin wants to see you, sir. I told him you was busy."

"I am busy," Taggart said to Fagin.

Fagin quickly untangled himself and got to his feet. "I want a word with you, Taggart. And you know what about."

Taggart sighed. "Oh, shit, it was bound to happen sooner or later anyhow. Go on in." He looked down at Blanchard. "Jesus Christ! Get on your feet, Sergeant. You look stupid laying there like that!"

"Yes, sir!" Blanchard popped up into the position of attention.

Taggart walked into his office behind Fagin. "Get a drink. I got some Irish whiskey in the cabinet."

Fagin's temper calmed a bit. "When did you get that?"

"When I figured it was the only way to keep you from drinking up all my scotch," Taggart said. "Now let's clear the air on this Black Eagle situation."

Fagin poured himself a tumbler of liquor. He walked to a chair in front of the general's desk and sat down. After a quick gulp, he said, "Let's start with the subject of those jeep-mounted recoil rifles. The 106-millimeter jobbers to be exact."

Taggart shrugged. "They didn't come through."

"I know goddamned well they didn't," Fagin said. "I learned that after I shot off my big stupid mouth about 'em to Falconi and his guys then found out from Sergeant Matsuno that a load of throw-away rocket launchers had arrived in their place."

"Those LAWS are damn good weapons," Taggart said.

"They're not as good as 106's," Fagin pointed out.

"They're better'n nothing," Taggart countered.

"Yeah. And I suppose I should be glad that Falconi didn't have to go out there and face Soviet tanks with his bare hands."

Taggart shrugged. "You know how logistics get fucked up."

"What we're talking about goes a hell of a lot further than just supply forms and procedures," Fagin said. "We're talking about a dozen guys going face-to-face with enemy armor!"

"I know the score," Taggart said. "My own G3 wrote the OPLAN." Then he quickly added, "And my G4 wrote the supply annex, okay?"

"Taggart, it's bad enough when I knowingly show up at the Black Eagle briefings a day late and a dollar short," Fagin says. "I realize the fortunes of war don't always shine on the deserving. I can handle that. And so can Falconi. But when I'm told one thing and turn around and promise it to the Black Eagles, then it falls through . . ." He let it hang.

Taggart got up and mixed his own drink. After a deep swallow, he turned and looked at the CIA operative. "Fagin, the last word I had received when you and Andrea flew out to Nui Dep was that those damned jeeps and the recoilless rifles would be delivered right behind you." He took another healthy swig. "Hell, that's why I arranged a C-130 to take the new guys out to Nui Dep. If I knew that only a crate of LAWS was going along I could have dispatched 'em in an H-34 chopper."

Fagin believed the man. Taggart was a pushy son

of a bitch, a hard-headed bastard, and a completely rotten swine. But he was not a liar. Fagin nodded his understanding. "So what happened?"

"It wasn't a fuck up," Taggart said softly.

Fagin couldn't speak for a few moments. When he finally did, his voice was subdued and strained. "Are you telling me that those jeeps were purposely taken out of the mission?"

"Yeah," Taggart answered.

"You mean that some staff asshole said, 'Take away the jeeps and recoilless rifles on that anti-tank mission'? Is that what you're saying?"

"I'm afraid so," Taggart said.

"Why?"

"For the worst goddamned reason imaginable," Taggart replied.

"Fill me in," Fagin said. "I've got a hell of an imagination. There's no telling what might jump into my mind."

"From the expression on your face, it already has," Taggart said.

"Are we talking pressure from the home front affecting tactical decisions now?"

"Exactly," Taggart said.

Fagin treated himself to a desperate gulp of liquor. "God have mercy on those poor bastards!"

Andrea Thuy paid off the taxi and hurried across the sidewalk to the door of her apartment building. The concierge, an elderly Vietnamese man who was a retired *sergeant-chef* of the colonial army, greeted her warmly. *"Chao Lan* Thuy!"

"Chao ong!" Andrea replied. "How are you today?"

"Toi manh!"

"That is good to hear. Has my friend gone out at

all today?" Andrea asked.

"Only for a short walk," the old man replied. "I warned her not to go far. Euros and Africans attract Viet Cong assassins in the city as well as in the jungle. Fortunately, she listened to me and returned about an hour ago."

"Thank you," Andrea said. She went to the stairs and ascended them to the second floor. Stopping at her door, she rapped out a signal.

"Are you delivering the groceries?" came a question from the interior.

"The refrigerator is already full," Andrea replied.

The door opened, showing Uzuri Mwanamke standing there. She was a tall, lovely black woman. Although slim, she was large-breasted with curvaceous hips. "Come in, Andrea," she said. "And I do feel a bit silly playing those word code games simply to open the door."

"It's safer, believe me," Andrea said. "And where is the pistol?"

"I left it in the drawer," Uzuri said. "I may force myself to observe your security precautions for safety's sake, but I shan't handle a weapon."

"Suit yourself," Andrea said. "I prefer survival to getting blown away by a VC agent." She reached in her pocket, pulling out Calvin Culpepper's letter. "This is what you're waiting for."

"He answered me?" Uzuri asked, suddenly excited. She took the letter and walked over to the sofa. Sitting down she looked at the folded paper. "I'm afraid to open it, Andrea. What does it say?"

"Uzuri! I didn't read it," Andrea exclaimed.

"How did he seem when you mentioned me?" Uzuri asked. "Tell me the truth please! I must force myself to deal with the reality of the situation even if it breaks my heart!"

"He seemed pleasantly surprised that you had an interest in him," Andrea answered. "Remember? That's what you told me to tell him."

"Wasn't he happy? Ecstatic? Overjoyed?" Her expression turned. "Or angry and disgusted?"

"Sergeant First Class Calvin Culpepper is a cool, logical, highly intelligent, professional soldier," Andrea said. "He is not the type to leap up and click his heels and shout with glee. I simply said you cared about him and he said that he was under the impression that you considered him no less than a raping, baby killer."

Uzuri frowned. "I never, never said that to him."

Andrea shrugged. "Sometimes our words and conduct give the wrong impressions." She gestured. "Go ahead and read the letter."

Uzuri slowly unfolded the paper. "His penmanship is excellent."

"To hell with the penmanship," Andrea said. "It's the words that are important."

"Of course." Uzuri read the message written there. Her eyes carefully scanned each line. When she was finished, she refolded the paper and put it in her blouse pocket.

"It couldn't have been too bad," Andrea said. "You're keeping it."

"He very politely inquires after my health," Uzuri said. "He hopes my work is going nicely and that my family back in Uganda is well." Uzuri was silent for a moment, then she began to sob. "Oh, Andrea! He hates me!"

Andrea sat down beside her, putting her arms around Uzuri's shaking shoulders. "Now, my dear. You must remember that Calvin Culpepper is not a demonstrative person. I'm sure that when you two are able to get together, you'll find him much warmer and nicer."

Uzuri regained control of herself. "I—I hope so."

"Don't you worry," Andrea said. "Now I'll fix us a nice supper. How does fish and rice sound to you?"

"Quite nice," Uzuri replied.

Andrea stood up. "You'll have to excuse me for awhile this evening, Uzuri. I have to spend a little time at the office."

"Of course. I cannot let my personal problems interfere with your professional life."

"Now cheer up! We'll have a nice meal."

Chuck Fagin, drunk as a lord, poured the last of the whiskey into his glass. He tossed the empty bottle away and put his feet up on his desk. His office was empty and dark, the only light coming in was from the distant control tower at Peterson Field. He sipped the drink slowly, his mind only slightly numbed despite the recent hours of heavy drinking.

Two more empties were laying on the floor, giving evidence of the binge he was on. Fagin shook his head slowly as the black thoughts that filled his head swirled around in his alcohol-fogged brain.

"Goddamn—goddamn—goddamn—" he kept saying over and over.

He suddenly heard the outer door open. It closed, then the familiar sound of Andrea Thuy's footsteps approached his door. She rapped on it.

"Go 'way!" he mumbled.

"What?"

"Go 'way! Go far 'way!"

Andrea let herself in. She flipped on the lights, then gasped when she spotted Fagin. She had never seen him in such a deplorable, drunken condition. "Chuck Fagin! What's gotten in to you?"

"Andrea," he said. "Andrea. Andrea." He put his feet down and struggled to stand up. After two attempts he made it. "Andrea."

"Yes, Chuck?"

"They sent the Black Eagles on a mission," he said.

"I know," Andrea replied. "I was there, remember?"

"I talked to Taggart about it," Fagin said. "And he gave me the official word on the mission."

"What's the official word, Chuck?" she asked.

"Falconi and the guys—"

"Yes, Chuck?"

He started the sentence again. "Falconi and the guys aren't expected to come back."

CHAPTER 5

Archie Dobbs, fifty meters out in front of the rest of the detachment, held up his hand and signaled a halt.

Although the terrain was open and visibility was relatively easy, he wanted to make sure that no smudges that appeared in the distance would turn out to be enemy troops or vehicles instead of harmless treelines or other natural features. He raised his binoculars to his eyes and gazed through them at the distant horizon.

This had been how the Detachment spent that day and the previous one. Moving slowly, cautiously across the tabletop flat terrain, they sought out an enemy that could be anywhere within thousands of square miles. The Black Eagles played a game of move, wait, look, and listen — then move on again to repeat the routine.

The Prick-Six radio hanging over his shoulder crackled to life with Lieutenant Colonel Robert Falconi's voice. "Scout, this is Falcon. Over."

Archie pulled the radio up to his ear. "Falcon, this is Scout. There's still plenty of nothing ahead. I spotted something ahead but it looks like another bunch o' trees around a creek. Over."

"Roger. Let's halt at the place for a rest. Out."

Archie was glad they would be taking a break. Tired by the monotony of travel across the plains country, he resumed what he'd been doing doggedly on this second day of the mission: leading the Black Eagle Detachment across the wide, empty expanse of the Cammon Plateau. With his uncanny sense of direction, Archie had to refer to his compass only on rare occasions. He plodded due north toward the hazy vision of vegetation on the horizon.

Back in the column the men moved lethargically under the hot sun. Noise discipline was enforced — and effectively kept to the maximum by Sergeant Major Top Gordon — so there was no unnecessary talking. The only sounds coming from the Detachment were heavy breathing and the scuffle of the men's rubber-soled boots on the hard-packed dirt of the plains country.

Alpha Fire Team, under Ray Swift Elk, led the main body behind Archie Dobbs. Falconi occupied the center of the formation and the Bravos formed the tail of the Black Eagle line. The last man, marine Sergeant Loco Padilla, turned around now and then to walk backward and keep a wary eye to the rear. It would have been embarrassing — and quite fatal — to have enemy troops sneak up on the tail of the column.

Each man felt awkward with the six LAWS rockets attached to his field gear. Although not real heavy, they were a bit clumsy to manage since it was impossible to tie them down securely.

The two men who were equipped differently, Steve Matsuno and Gunnar Olson, kept their M16 rifles slung over their shoulders while they carried one of the anti-tank weapons in case of a mechanized attack. In the event of an armored assault, they would be the men of the hour, taking on the steel monsters while the others in the Detachment provided them covering fire.

But Archie Dobbs wasn't worried about tanks. The vehicles were noisy and easy to spot. The scout was more concerned with the creek ahead. He wanted that breather and a chance to sit down with Lieutenant Colonel Falconi to plan out the rest of the day's walk. They also had to decide where and when they would call a halt for the day. They needed a place that was secure enough to make a good base camp, yet located in an area that offered the best opportunity to run some night patrols.

One of Falconi's basic military philosophies was that active patrolling activities not only guaranteed the enemy couldn't surprise you, it gave indication of the best opportunities to mount an offense.

Archie glanced back and could barely see Blue Richards leading the rest of the column. He turned to the front and stepped up his pace. The creek was closer, showing the trees and tall grass growing around its lush banks. Cool shade and cold water would be waiting for a group of hot, thirsty troops. Archie pulled one of his canteens from its carrier and gulped down the last of the luke-warm water in it. He licked his lips and spat in anticipation of the delicious, refreshing drinks waiting for him at the waterway.

Abruptly the placid scene turned to shit.

The Pathet Lao riflemen suddenly raised up over the cover of the creek bank and cut loose with rapid semi-automatic shooting.

Archie dropped to the ground, letting his canteen go, as he took up a prone firing position and blasted back.

Falconi heard the exchange of shots. He and his

men were in a wide-open space without cover or even a dip in the ground to use for protection. He could order a retreat to attempt a hasty escape or he could go forward. The Black Eagle commander made up his mind in a split second.

"Alphas left! Bravos right! As skirmishers! Go!"

The men spread out in a single line facing the enemy. Performing on the run, the two LAWS men substituted their rifles for the little rockets. Firing broke out immediately, the rounds zipping over and past Archie.

"Grenadiers!" Falconi yelled. "Air bursts!"

Paulo Garcia and Loco Padilla, each with an M203 grenade launcher attached to their M16s, went into action with the explosive-throwing weapons. Although running, they managed to quickly shove M397 air burst grenades into the breeches. Hastily aiming, they estimated the range and each cut loose. The devices were blown out of the launcher barrels and arced up into the air. They went beyond the creek, hitting the ground then bounding up to explode. Spurts of dirt flew up and some of the vegetation was cut from the higher branches of the trees along the waterway.

Archie Dobbs, meanwhile, was still returning fire while crawling backward toward the Detachment. He knew they were advancing, because the sound of the firing behind him was getting louder. But he had no time to look rearward to judge their actual position. Any letup on his part would give the Pathet Lao ahead of him the chance to take careful aim at him.

Blue Richards and Calvin Culpepper were the first two to reach Archie's position. As they closed in on the scout, Calvin yelled, "Get up now, Archie. We're here!"

"Jesus!" Archie exclaimed getting to his feet. "Am I

glad to have company!"

The three men, forming the front of the "V" formation of the attack, continued to move forward. Their combined fire at a close range made the enemy soldiers become wary. The Pathet Lao shooting decreased slightly as they began to duck their heads amidst the ricochets and flying slugs zipping their way.

Falconi, not knowing the extent of the positions they were attacking, didn't want his whole effort concentrated on a frontal assault. "Ky! Gunnar!" he shouted. "Come with me!"

He led the two Black Eagles obliquely off the line of assault, heading for the right hand side of the battle. Ky, the short little ex-Viet Cong, ran as fast as his short legs would go in order to keep up with the two taller Americans.

When the trio was fifty yards away from the main action, Falconi quickly veered inward. He rushed to the creek. Firing on full-automatic in case there were other Pathet Lao there, he leaped over the bank, landing in the knee-deep water.

Both Gunnar, and Ky, as combat veterans, knew what the colonel was doing. It was a classic outflanking movement that would take them right up the unprotected side of the defenders. All three charged down the bank, splashing through the muddy water. When they caught sight of the first enemy troops, they opened up with rapid shots.

The first Pathet Lao to fall didn't even know what hit them. The next to die, had only a chance to look toward the sound of the surprise attack before they were blasted into that great communist cell meeting in the sky.

The main group of Black Eagles suddenly appeared on the bank. Between their fusillades and that of the three flankers, the rest of the enemy unit collapsed under the storm of steel-jacketed slugs, their bullet-torn bodies falling into the water, turning it from brown to red.

"Cease fire!" Top Gordon bellowed.

A sudden vacuum of silence fell over the scene. The Black Eagles on the bank looked down on Falconi, Gunnar and Ky. Then they studied the bodies of the dead Pathet Lao looking grotesque in the shallow creek.

"I ain't drinking that fucking water," Archie said. "Them sonofabitches are bleeding in it."

"Hold my weapon," Paulo Garcia said to Steve Matsuno. He jumped down into the narrow water-way. As the intelligence sergeant of the Detachment, he was interested in what information could be learned from the cadavers. He went to each one, pulling the dead man up on the muddy bank. He went through pockets, pulling out soggy documents and tossing them back up on the bank. "Can you read any of this, Ky?" he asked.

Ky Luyen shrugged. "It not my language, Paulo. But I see what I can do."

While Ray Swift Elk and Top Gordon arranged the rest of the men in a defensive position in case of a counter-attack, Paulo and Ky went through the soggy papers. They painstakingly unfolded each one, doing their best not to tear it. Ky looked carefully at them, shaking his head. "These are in Meo language," Ky said apologetically. He picked up one from another group. "Same same. So sorry about that." He looked at a couple of more. "Hey! Look!"

"You found something?" Paulo asked.

"Yes. Look, Paulo. I can't read writing but look at picture."

Paulo took the sopping wet document. "Jesus!" He

58

stood up. "Colonel Falconi, sir!"

Falconi left the others and joined the two intelligence gatherers. "What've you got there?"

"We can't read the writing, but look what one of these bastards doodled on this paper," Paulo said.

Falconi emitted a low whistle. "Doodled, hell! That's a pretty damned good sketch of a Russian T-55 tank."

"Yeah," Paulo said. "I guess ol' Chuck Fagin was right. This goddamned place is crawling with them."

Ky went through some more papers. "Here is little book. Different writing. But I no can read her. Sorry."

Falconi walked over and took the publication. "I can read it, Ky. It's in Russian."

"What is it?" Paulo asked.

"It's a Soviet army field manual," Falconi said. "A most interesting subject—'Combined Tank-Infantry Tactics'."

Paulo summed up his reaction with one word: "Shit!"

"Ky," Falconi said. "Fetch Swift Elk and Top over here. Then join the others on the perimeter."

"You bet, *Trung-Ta!*" He scurried away in quick obedience.

"I might as well go too, sir," Paulo Garcia said. "There ain't nothing left for me to do here."

"Right, Paulo," Falconi said. "Nice intel work, Marine."

"Semper Fi, semper on the ball, sir," Paulo said, returning to the Detachment.

Moments later, the team leaders reported to the detachment commander. "Ky says you want to see us *mau len,* sir," Top said.

"Yeah," Falconi answered. "We've found a Russian manual on tank-infantry tactics. The Pathet-Lao that carried it could no doubt read and understand every

59

word in the goddamned book. And I'm sure he wasn't the only one."

"Any evidence they were in training on the subject?" Ray Swift Elk asked.

"Right," Falconi answered. "We found some handwritten stuff and one of 'em had a drawing of a T-55 tank."

Ray Swift Elk shifted his M16 in his hands. "In other words, we'll go up against more than tanks. There'll be infantry support with the armor."

"I'm afraid so," Falconi said.

Top spat. "That goddamned Fagin never tells us enough! The sonofabitch really pisses me off sometimes."

"It does make the job tougher," Falconi admitted. "Going against tanks was bad enough. Having to deal with supporting infantry is going to triple the asshole-pucker factor."

"It'll make the mission damned near impossible," Ray Swift Elk said.

"Yeah," Falconi said. "But we've never quit no matter how fucked up the OPLANs they gave us. But this new information will change the tactical situation entirely. We'll have to not only cover our LAWS men during battle, but keep enemy foot troops at bay, too."

Falconi looked down at the dead Pathet Lao, their blood and bodily fluids fouling the creek. "We have another problem right now, however. And we must deal with it immediately. That enemy outfit undoubtedly has some friends nearby. We don't want them to catch us flat-footed. Let's get the hell out of here."

"But where, sir?" Top Gordon asked. He gestured at the open, flat terrain that surrounded them. "There's not enough concealment out there to give cover to a skinny snake."

"The only thing we can do is move off to the

northwest," Falconi said. "According to the OPLAN that should take us farther away from the main Pathet Lao troop concentrations."

"Fuck the OPLAN!" Swift Elk exclaimed. "The goddamned thing was wrong about enemy tactics. We might as well figure it's wrong about their positions, too."

"Lieutenant," Falconi said coldly and formally. "We don't have any choice."

Swift Elk sighed. "I guess not."

"Should we saddle 'em up and move 'em out, sir?" Sergeant Major Top Gordon asked.

"You bet," Falconi said. "Let's do like the old shepherd and get the flock outta here."

The two officers and the sergeant major jumped over the narrow creek to the other side. As they walked over to the men, a distant rumbling sounded in the distance.

"Thunder?" Top asked.

Archie Dobbs, standing up with his binoculars, stared out toward the horizon. "Thunder, hell! I see tanks. Big bastards!" He looked for a few more moments. "And infantry, for Chrissake! There's supporting infantry with the armor!"

Falconi's voice was calm. "Let's get back to the creek, guys. It might be messy with dead Pathet Lao, but right now it's the only salvation we got."

"Move it! Quickly!" Top Gordon shouted. "The man that stays up here, *dies* up here!"

CHAPTER 6

"Spread it out, you team leaders!"

Falconi's shouted orders caused Ray Swift Elk and Top Gordon to quickly readjust their men's fire positions along the creek bank. In their haste at forming up, the Black Eagles had instinctively situated themselves close together. The members of the detachment quickly — and wisely — readjusted their firing stations under Swift Elk and Top's not too gentle verbal prodding.

"Spread it out!" Top yelled, physically shoving Ky Luyen one way and Gunnar Olson the other. "What's the matter? Are you two guys in love or something?"

"Hell no!" Gunnar replied as he quickly obeyed the sergeant major. "Think what that would do to our security clearances."

"Knock off the wisecracks, Olson," Top snapped. "Look to the front and see what's going on."

The enemy was five hundred yards away.

The senior non-commissioned officer turned to the other men. "Grab them croaked Reds and heave 'em up out of the water onto the bank in front of you," Top ordered. "They'll give you some cover and you don't have to stumble all over them stiffs."

The bodies of the dead Pathet Lao were hauled out of the water and pushed out to the front to form a shallow barrier. There weren't many of them, but the small protection afforded by the cadavers was better than nothing.

Blue Richards settled one corpse into place, then noted the man's eyes—unseeing but wide open—seemed to stare at him. Wincing, he turned the dead Pathet Lao's head toward the other direction.

The two men of the hour—Gunnar Olson and Steve Matsuno—occupied the center of each team. All the men had taken their LAWS off their packs and deposited them with the two who had been designated as the official anti-tank team.

"Gunnar and Steve, listen up," Falconi said. "I want you two rocketeers to concentrate on those tanks. At this point we don't know how many of them are out there, but they all belong to you. Don't sweat the infantry around them. We'll take care of the foot soldiers. You'll be covered. Any questions?"

"No, sir!" Steve Matsuno said. He held a LAWS, primed and ready, on his shoulder.

Gunnar, also prepared for the coming battle, grinned. "I like that word."

"What word?" Loco Padilla near him asked.

"Rocketeers," Gunnar replied. "It sounds real fancy, don't it? Like grenadiers or musketeers."

"How about elephant ears?" Loco asked grinning.

Top Gordon barked at them. "Knock off the shit! We're just about to be up to our asses in Pathet Lao and Russian tanks, and you're cracking stupid jokes."

"Sergeant Major," Loco said. "It's the only thing that's keeping me from crying."

Further comment was interrupted by a shout from Archie, who had positioned himself out ahead of the others as a one-man outpost. "There's two tanks in front and they're coming fast." He emphasized the seriousness of the situation by jumping up and running back to the creek as fast as he could. He dived over the stacked dead, crashing into Blue Richards.

Blue was irritated. "First I got a croaked Red starin' me in the face, then you jump on top of me. How about watchin' it, Archie?"

"Sorry, Blue," Archie said, getting up out of the water. "But I was as close to them tanks as I wanted to be. They ain't more'n four hundred yards away."

"You're gonna be a lot closer," Blue said. "They're comin' on fast!"

Gunnar, preparing to go into action, suddenly remembered that hitting the tank from the front wasn't the best method of destroying it. Unfortunately, that was the only target offered at the time. "Steve!" he hollered over at the other rocketeer. "What do we shoot at? The turret or hull?"

"Neither one," Steve Matsuno yelled back. "Go for the treads."

"Right or left?"

Top Gordon interrupted. "Either goddamned one, goddamn it, Gunnar!"

"Yes, Sergeant Major!"

By that time, the attacking enemy was three hundred yards away.

"Open fire!" Falconi yelled.

Ten M16s suddenly spit spurts of flame and slugs toward the steadily approaching Pathet Lao. A few of the enemy soldiers either pitched forward to the ground or staggered backward before falling as the Black Eagle fusillades took their toll. But others, ignoring their unlucky comrades, moved forward to fill the gaps.

Malpractice McCorkel shoved another magazine into his weapon, looking out at the falling enemy. "Them bastards don't mind dying, do they?" he commented before resuming his steady single-shot attempts at reducing their number.

Over in the Alpha Assault Team, Steve Matsuno judged the time was right. He carefully aimed the LAWS on the left hand tread of the tank on his side of the line. He pressed the firing boot and his weapon blasted out its two-and-a-quarter pound rocket. As the backblast blew away a portion of the creek bank behind the firer, the projectile streaked out across the open space between him and the moving target. It struck the far side of the armored vehicle, bouncing off to explode a few meters high and to the right. A half dozen Pathet Lao infantrymen died in its hot detonation, but the tank pressed on relentlessly.

"Damn me for an asshole!" Steve exclaimed, disgusted with himself. He threw the spent tube down and grabbed a charged one.

Gunnar Olson decided it was his turn. He drew a careful bead on the tank coming his way. Taking a deep breath, he held it for an instant as his hand almost lovingly tightened on the firing boot.

Ka-Boom!

Mud, dirt, and hunks of a Pathet Lao body left in the rear flew up in the air from the backblast in a mixture of dirty water and blood.

Gunnar's rocket missed the tread but hit dead center on the hull. The resulting explosion threw the heavy vehicle off course and it came to a halt.

Falconi quickly examined the damage through his binoculars. "You penetrated the armor, Gunnar! Nice shooting!"

"Prob'ly killed the driver," Top surmised. He'd faced North Korean and Chinese armored units in the Korean War. The old sergeant knew from experience what was going on inside the hull of the tank. "They're shook up and their ears is ringing, but the bastards' weaponry is still operative."

As if to prove the sergeant major right, the big turret cannon boomed out, its shell shrieking overhead to explode fifty yards to the rear.

Ray Swift Elk wiped at the sweat coursing down his copper-colored face. "If they get our range—"

Now the other tank cut loose with its artillery. Once again, the horrible ripping sound of a flying shell streaked over the heads of the Detachment.

"Fuck this shit!" Archie said. He slung his rifle over his shoulder and sloshed down the creek to Steve Matsuno's location. Grabbing one of the LAWS, Archie continued his hasty trip down the waterway. When he'd gone a hundred yards, he leaped out on the enemy side and ran fast and low straight ahead.

The intrepid scout managed to make it to a point almost even with the tanks when he was finally spotted by the enemy. Numerous Pathet Lao, enraged by his brashness, turned their AK47 assault rifles and blasted away.

Archie damned them, their mammies, their grannies, and their baby sisters as he continued to run toward a favorable position. When he reached a good spot, he feigned being hit. Stumbling and doubling over, he fell to the ground. The incoming fire quickly lifted as the enemy turned their attention back to the tenacious defenders in the creek.

Archie rolled over into a prone firing position grasping the LAWS. He cocked the firing pin by pulling the recocking latch rod assembly forward. After removing the pull pin he rotated the rear cover downward. This allowed the front cover and sling assembly to drop off.

Now several of the Pathet Lao noticed he was moving around again. Once again 7.62-millimeter bullets zipped his way, kicking up dirt around him and zipping through the air around his head.

Archie spat as he extended the launcher into readiness for firing and removed the safety pin. "Now," he said to himself, "I'm gonna kick ass."

The incoming fire increased markedly as more of the enemy finally noted the lone man facing them from their flank had some sort of weapon with him that seemed a threat to the nearest tank.

Archie depressed the firing boot, feeling the weapon's instant loss of weight as the rocket flew out of the tube. In less than a second, the round hit the side of the tank. It exploded, sending shards of metal and hunks of the tread flying out to slice into the nearby Pathet Lao infantry.

The tank came to an abrupt halt and all firing from it immediately ceased. The vehicle was quiet, with wisps of smoke coming from the turret cannon and the hole where the rocket had gone in.

Back at the main position, Gunnar Olson had not given up. He carefully prepared another LAWS of his own. He calmly and deliberately sighted in on the space between the hull and turret on the tank he had previously damaged. Its crew had added the machine guns to the efforts of the booming cannon whose shells were closing in on the embattled Black Eagle Detachment.

Finally satisfied that he was right on the target, Gunnar pressed down on the firing boot. Once more a roaring blast was followed by a streaking rocket.

The projectile struck true, even causing the heavy turret to leap a bit as it penetrated its armor. All firing ceased as the top hatch opened up. A screaming tanker, wrapped in flames, climbed out of the vehicle and leaped to the ground. He ran a few yards before finally collapsing.

The enemy's armored attack was over. Both vehicles were out of action.

"What the hell are you staring at?" Falconi demanded of the Black Eagles. "Archie is still out there! As skirmishers, move forward!"

The Detachment clamored out of the creek and began a quick-paced advance toward the enemy. Needing no urging, Paulo Garcia and Loco Padilla cranked their M203 grenade launchers into action. Their quick firing resulted in six M433 grenades being launched in lazy arcs that soared upward toward the Pathet Lao. After reaching the zenith of their trajectory, the grenades sped earthward, striking among the now confused enemy. The explosions, each with a bursting radius of five meters, erupted inside the Pathet Lao ranks. Although overlapping, these areas of death covered two hundred and twenty-five square feet of blasting, tearing death.

The Pathet Lao, demoralized by the unthinkable, awful fate of the two Russian tanks with them, put up a spiritless defense. Even the battle fever of those screaming zealots cooled down under the onslaught of the Black Eagles' military professionalism.

After discarding the used portion of the LAWS, Archie had turned to his M16 now that the anti-tank weapon was used up. He slipped the selector on his rifle to full-automatic. Hosing streams of 5.56-millimeter slugs, he crammed five full twenty-round magazines into his weapon.

The Red infantrymen, looking at their dozens of fallen comrades and the smoking hulks of the destroyed tanks, finally decided the battle was over. No order to retreat was given. The route began when a couple of more hesitant soldiers who had been hanging back, simultaneously turned and raced to the rear. A few near them thought the example they set was exemplary, so they joined the unannounced retreat.

A young non-commissioned officer caught a glimpse of the fleeing men. He assumed some higher-ranker had given the order to pull out, so he screamed orders at his section. Quickly—and gratefully—obeying him, the men also raced toward safety.

Within the short space of sixty-seconds, the entire Pathet Lao unit was on the run. The Black Eagles stepped up their own pace, trying to close with the little fleeing bastards, but Falconi only allowed them to go a hundred yards before he shouted to Ray Swift Elk and Top Gordon to halt their men and bring them back to the tanks.

The battle ended as the Reds finally raced out of range of the Detachment's rifles. Archie Dobbs, the exertion of his single-handed effort finally catching up with him, walked slowly back to the Detachment.

"Nice going, Archie!" Loco Padilla shouted to him.

"Good shooting," Paulo Garcia added.

"Do that again," Falconi said, "and I'll put you so far back in the stockade they'll have to pump fresh air and sunshine in to you."

Archie, puzzled, shot a quick glance over at his commanding officer. "What the hell, sir?"

Top Gordon entered the picture bellowing. "And if it was up to me, I'd railroad your ass into Leavenworth."

"Gimme a break!" Archie protested. "I risked my ass to go out there and—"

"No!" Falconi snapped. "You risked *our* asses to go out there and get that tank. Gunnar and Steve were assigned as the anti-tank team."

"They missed!" Archie argued.

"Gunnar got a good hit the second time and Steve was beginning to find the mark," Falconi said. "Your job was to provide firepower at the infantry to keep them off our backs while the LAWS guys did their thing."

The sudden logic of what was being said to him finally sunk in. Archie nodded his head. "Yes, sir. I fucked up."

"Sort of," Falconi said. Then he grinned. "But you'd have really fucked up if you'd missed that tank."

"It won't happen again, sir," Archie said embarrassed.

"That's good enough for me, Archie," Falconi said. He turned and motioned the other men to gather around. "The big question has been answered now. Not only did we keep 'em off our backs this time, we learned that it is possible to kill tanks with those LAWS."

"And tankers," Calvin Culpepper said pointing to the still smoking, charred cadaver of the man who had climbed out of the armored vehicle while swathed in flames. "And there's more of 'em still inside there."

"Right," Falconi agreed. "But we're on foot in open country, relatively inexperienced in this sort of mission, and we're facing an enemy that can pop up anywhere, at anytime. Today was a damned good indication of that."

"Orders, sir?" Ray Swift Elk asked.

"We'll move due west of here until dark," Falconi said. "Then we'll settle in for the night. I want fifty percent alert at all times during the hours of darkness. We won't get much sleep, but nobody can sneak up on us that way."

"What about tomorrow, sir?" Top Gordon asked. "What's on the agenda."

Falconi indicated the battle debris of blasted armor and dead bodies scattered around them. "More of this shit."

CHAPTER 7

A MATTER OF PRIORITIES

Those cold, impersonal words on the official G3 Situation Report issued by SOG Operations cut deep into Andrea Thuy's heart like the thrust of a cold, steel *mot con dao* blade.

The awful meaning behind the statement was that for a period of time, the Black Eagle Detachment, out on an operation in Laos, would be left completely unsupported and cut-off. In truth, they were abandoned. Although not ignored through callous disregard, the predicament was keenly resented by those closest to them.

Chuck Fagin's reaction to the news was typical of his Irish temperament:

"How much fucking time, you fucking idiots?"

Nobody knew. The staff officers shrugged, the staff non-commissioned officers looked the other way, and the enlisted clerks rolled their eyes in disgust at this monumental military snafu.

The only thing anyone knew for sure was that politics played a big part of the situation. With the war's unpopularity growing to clamoring proportions back on the home front, the number of casualties suffered by average G.I.s had to be kept to the absolute minimum. When a big operation involving draftee soldiers was launched in the Central Highlands, every source of supply, ammunition, transport, and personnel was dedicated to the mission. In every case—*every* case—that meant pulling resources from other programs even if it meant cutting those projects deadly short of what they needed.

A group of professional soldiers, sailors, and marines like the Black Eagles, while certainly not considered expendable in any ordinary sense of the word, could be put at great risk without having to sweat any unpleasant reaction from the brass, congress, or the public. After all, these were fighters-by-choice who had volunteered for the dangerous jobs they undertook. Nobody pulled them off of farms, out of schools, or away from their mama's breasts. The Black Eagles asked for trouble and got it. Not too much of a chance for sympathy from John Q. Public in a case like that.

Therefore, the top dogs pulled away the aircraft and logistical support the Black Eagles needed in their latest mission of destroying Soviet tanks of the NVA on the Cammon Plateau in Laos.

In other words: there would be no resupply until further notice.

Chuck Fagin's rampage produced nothing. In the end he wasn't too surprised, but he was still madder than hell. With SOG standing firm because of pressures from higher up, the stubborn CIA officer turned to his own agency. Again he hit a dead end. With no funds available it would be impossible to get the airplane and weaponry the Black Eagles needed.

No organization could commit a transport aircraft, the gasoline to run it, or the personnel to man it unless the money spent on those expensive items was reimbursed. Without recouping any monies spent, they would be unable to run future operations. The general public may think that the military and intelligence services simply run around crazy and happy with taxpayer dollars, but the facts of the matter are that they are under tight budgetary controls.

While Chuck Fagin frantically sought some solution in the paperwork nightmare, Andrea Thuy prepared her friend Uzuri Mwanamke for the worst. The beautiful black woman from Uganda, Africa, was still a guest in her apartment.

That incident took place on the evening the bad news was first given to her and Fagin. Andrea spent a long day doing follow-up letters and even phone calls on the appeals that Fagin was creating. It was almost ten o'clock when Andrea finally got back to the apartment. When she walked through the door, the expression on her face showed that she was upset by more than simple physical fatigue.

Uzuri, a most perceptive young woman, knew that something was very seriously wrong. She smiled bravely and walked over, taking Andrea's arm. "Sit down, *rafiki*. I can see you are troubled. Let me make you some nice, hot tea."

"Yes, Uzuri," Andrea said. "Thank you. That would be wonderful. While you're putting the pot on the stove, I shall take a quick shower."

A quarter of an hour later, both women were seated on the large over-stuffed sofa in the living room of the apartment. Andrea, without speaking, enjoyed the first sips of the freshly brewed drink. Uzuri, waiting with the patience so universal in her native Africa, also remained silent.

Finally, when Andrea felt more controlled, she spoke carefully. "Uzuri, there is something I must talk to you about. But please understand. I cannot tell you everything, nor can I answer any probing questions."

Now Uzuri understood. "It involves my Calvin, does it not, *rafiki?*"

"Yes."

Uzuri displayed a brave smile. "Has something bad happened to him, Andrea?"

Andrea reached out and patted her friend on the hand. "We have no such bad news. It is a situation brought on by circumstances dictated by the character of this war. That is all I can say."

"But he is in great danger, is he not?" Uzuri asked.

"Yes," Andrea replied. "You figured that out quite quickly."

"In my land, where my people have lived since the beginning of the world, there is a thing called *kiinimacho*. It is the art of using one's greatest spiritual powers to probe into the realities of the physical world. The old people say that once there were great practitioners of this craft who could go beyond investigation. They could actually see into the future and even change things. Some are blessed with such skill they could enter the dreams of sleeping people. *Ajabu!* They were wonders!"

Andrea nodded. "There are such people like that in the legends of my own Oriental ancestors."

"I have no such powers, but I do have a great strength in being able to perceive circumstances without being told," Uzuri said. "I will concentrate and focus my spirit onto Calvin. That way I shall know if the spark of life is still within him."

"Do the same for Robert Falconi, will you, Uzuri?" Andrea asked.

Uzuri smiled sadly. *"Huzuni!* I cannot," she said. "I do not love him."

Andrea leaned toward her. "Then I shall do so. Show me how, Uzuri!"

The Ugandan woman sat down her cup of tea. "Settle back and close your eyes. What you are about to do is to concentrate more than you have ever done in your entire life . . ."

Chuck Fagin, scribbling on the tablet with a worn stub of a pencil, glanced up in angry frustration when the sound of loud banging on the door in the outer office interrupted his line of thought. It was midnight and he was tired, pissed-off, hungry, and pining for a stiff shot of whiskey.

"Fagin! Fagin!" It was Taggart.

And that irritated Fagin the most — the voice belonging to Brigadier General James Taggart. The officer's raspy speech made Fagin's Irish temper snap even faster than usual.

"What the hell's going on out there?" he shouted. He got up and walked from his own office into the reception area Andrea used. He opened the door.

Taggart brushed past him, barging in like he owned the place. "How're you doing, Fagin? C'mon into your office. I want to talk with you."

Fagin followed him back. "What's on your alleged mind, Taggart?"

The general carried a leather briefcase that he deposited on the CIA officer's desk before making himself at home on a chair by the door. "I was just thinking about you and thought I'd drop in to say 'hi'."

Fagin, puzzled by the apparent friendliness of the visit, glared suspiciously at the general. "What the fuck do you want, Taggart? If you're trying to hit me up for a loan, forget it! I already owe more than you could want to borrow."

Taggart grinned. The happy expression seemed alien on his craggy features. "Goddamn, boy! I just wanted to see my old pal. Anything wrong in that?"

Fagin sat down. "Nope."

"So how's the little lady?"

"I ain't married," Fagin said.

"No shit? I thought you were," Taggart said.

"I used to be," Fagin said. "But it's kind of hard to maintain a decent home life while running intelligence operations from the mountains in Eastern Europe to the swamps of Southeast Asia."

Taggart shook his head. "Tsk! Tsk! She just didn't understand you, did she?"

"She understood me alright," Fagin said. "She understood I thought she was a babbling bitch." He leaned back in his chair. "Hell, I remember one time—" He stopped talking. "What the hell is going on, Taggart. You ain't fooling nobody. Now I want you to level with me."

"There's no big deal, pal. I just wanted to see you," Taggart insisted.

"Taggart, you don't like me and I don't like you. So what the hell do we have to visit about?" Fagin snarled. "We'll be at each other's throats in another fifteen minutes of this sappy, sugary shit."

Taggart suddenly stood up. "Well, this has been swell, old buddy. Let's do it again sometime, huh?" He turned and performed a brisk exit.

Fagin sat dumbfounded for a couple of seconds. Then he noticed the briefcase. He grabbed it and rushed out the door. "Taggart! Taggart! You forgot something."

The general, out in the hall, turned. "What? I didn't bring anything with me."

"Sure you did, you dumb bastard," Fagin said displaying the leather case. "This."

"It's not mine."

"What the hell—"

"What's in it?" Taggart asked.

Fagin clicked the locks. The case opened, revealing that it was stuffed with American dollars. "Jesus!"

"Hey," Taggart said. "I wish it was mine, believe me."

"C'mon, Taggart! Of course—"

Taggart gazed directly into Fagin's eyes. "Look, pal. All my operating accounts are up to snuff, understand? Every damned dollar is accounted for to the boys in G1. On the books I'm a financial genius. So it must be your money."

Suddenly Fagin understood. The general had built up a surplus from the cash accounts used in clandestine operations. With his books juggled, every account was no doubt right up to snuff to the last red cent—on paper. Fagin grinned. "Thanks, Taggart."

"It's your money, pal. Maybe you can use it to help out Falconi and those goddamned pirates of his." Giving a little wave, he turned and continued his rapid walk down the hall. "Though they don't deserve a cent of it, if you ask me."

"I ain't asking you!" Fagin yelled happily. He went back to his office and spilled the contents of the briefcase over his desk. Counting quickly but accurately, he tallied up a total of fifty thousand dollars. "That son of a bitch!" Fagin crowed. "That goddamned son of a bitch!" He let out a whoop. "That goddamned, magnificent son of a bitch!" He pulled a cigar out of his pocket. "It's too bad I hate his guts." After lighting up, he dialed a number on his telephone. It rang several times before a sleepy Oriental man answered:

"A-lo?"

"Hello, Choy, you thief," Fagin said. "Go pull Donegan out of bed."

"Oh, no! He get plenty mad, Fagin. You betcha!" The voice was heavily accented.

Fagin yelled into the receiver. "Do what I tell you, you little fart face, or I'll come over there and kick your ass!"

"Better you kick my ass not Donegan," Choy said.

"He got a woman in there."

"Yeah?" Fagin asked. "Is she pretty?"

"No way, Fagin. Fat and ugly."

"That's what I figured," Fagin said. "That dumb bastard Donegan's got no taste."

The Oriental man's laughter filled the receiver. "You damned good and right about that, Fagin. You betcha!"

"Are you guys committed right now?"

"Oh, no!" Choy said. "We just finish up and come in from cold. We do a bit of R&R."

"That's great. So here's what I want you to do, Choy. Go up to the bedroom door, knock on it, and yell out that I got a job for him, okay?"

"I do that!"

"What kind of airplane do you guys have now?"

"Flying boat! Very nice. Go on land. Go on water."

"Is McKeever still his crew chief?"

"You betcha! And I'm number one navigator like always," Choy said.

"Yeah. You guys are a hunnerd percent Irish, ain't you?"

"You betcha!"

"Well, do like I say. And get McKeever, too. I've got a job that's gonna curl your hair. I'll see all three of you jokers at seven o'clock."

"You betcha!"

Fagin hung up. He looked at the piles of money scattered across his desk, thinking of Taggart.

"That magnificent son of a bitch!"

CHAPTER 8

Archie Dobbs walked gingerly down the ravine, stepping lightly to make sure he created no unnecessary noises. The Black Eagle Detachment scout was in his natural element. A born tracker with the instincts of a hunting wolf, he was reputed to be the best compass-and-map man in the United States Army. His sense of direction was as uncanny as his instinctive ability to sense danger.

After traveling fifty meters, Archie stopped. The scout listened carefully for a full minute before he eased up the side of the natural ditch and peered out over the expanse of the Cammon Plateau.

The terrain was bleak and empty.

No sign of life, other than a few flying birds, could be detected. The scout was particularly glad there were no enemy tanks present. Like the other Black Eagles, an unspoken but very real apprehension about facing those iron monsters again gnawed at his natural bravery. It was one thing to go against armor as part of a large conventional military effort, but quite another when you were a member of a small detachment facing them all alone in unfriendly territory.

Archie slid back to the bottom of the arroyo. He

looked back where Blue Richards of Swift Elk's Alpha Team crouched twenty-five meters away. Archie gave a high-sign letting him know everything was okay.

Moments later, Lieutenant Colonel Robert Falconi appeared from the middle of the column. He walked quickly but quietly forward until he joined the scout. "How does it look, Archie?"

"There's nothing stirring out there, sir," Archie said. "Best of all, I can't hear any tank engines. But that don't mean there ain't nobody like us crouching in a ditch on the other side."

They had reached both the time and place in the mission when a normally scheduled aerial logistics insertion was supposed to take place. Falconi checked his watch. "That supply drop is scheduled to take place in another half hour."

"That's what the OPORD says, sir," Archie said. "God only knows when the plane is gonna show up."

"I'm anxious to see the aircraft," Falconi said. "We can sure as hell use any goodies they deliver to us. But if there's any unfriendlies around when those supply parachutes blossom open, they're going to be attracted here like flies to spilled sugar."

Archie shrugged. "All we can do is give the recovery detail all the covering fire we can muster."

"Yeah. Then give them some more." Falconi nodded as he grabbed his radio. "Bravo, this is Falcon. Send the recovery party forward. Over."

"Roger, Falcon," came back Top Gordon's voice. "Out."

Minutes later Sergeant First Class Calvin Culpepper, followed by Ky Luyen and Loco Padilla, hurried up the natural ditch to join Falconi and Archie.

"We're set to go, sir," Calvin said. As the man in charge of the detail, he would be responsible for more than grabbing the dropped equipment and returning to the ravine. He also had to worry about his men's safety during the time they would be exposed to any potential enemy fire.

Once again Falconi went to his radio. "Alpha, this is Falcon. Move into position. Out."

There was only a slight rustling heard down that gully. A couple of minutes later, Sergeant Major Top Gordon led his men past the recovery detail to take up fighting posts farther down the gully. They passed the others with nods, the nervousness they felt hidden behind crooked grins and winks.

When Top Gordon was satisfied his men were in the best location, he radioed back to Falconi to report he was ready. "We're standing tall, Falcon," crackled the sergeant major's voice. "How long 'til the aircraft is due?"

"Twenty minutes," Falconi said. "Stand ready. Out."

Archie looked skyward. "I hope they're on time."

"They're never on time," Falconi said. "But they'll be showing up sometime today. We'll have to hang loose until the aircraft makes its appearance."

Chuck Fagin paid off the taxi, then slid out the door. He had taken the cab to a lower class Saigon neighborhood. The very moment he stepped up on the curb, dozens of street urchins surrounded him. Each child, his high-pitched voice squealing as loud as possible, yelled at the American:

"Hey! Shoe-shine, mister?"

"You look for girly-girly?"

"Want dope? I get you best stuff."

Fagin, knowing what sort of reception he would get, was prepared. He reached in his pocket and pulled out a handful of coins. He tossed the money straight up in the air and walked away. The kids scrambled among themselves to pick it up, fighting, yelling, and pushing in their excitement.

While the mini-riot continued, Fagin walked across the sidewalk and entered a gate that led to an apartment house courtyard. An old woman sat by one door watching a small child at play.

"*Chao ba,*" he greeted her. "*Dau nha* Donegan?"

Wordlessly, she pointed to an upstairs flat.

"*Cam on ba,*" he said, thanking her. The CIA man walked to the rickety staircase and went upstairs. Although there were several apartments, he knew that Tim Donegan would have rented the entire upper floor. Fagin went to the first door and banged on it. "Choy! Open up!" When there was no answer, he went to the next and repeated the attempt to get somebody. Finally, the fourth door opened.

A short, husky, tough-looking Chinese man answered the summons. "Hey, Fagin. Come in." He had a tough, pugilist's face, but it bore a friendly grin for the caller. "Good for to you see you again. You betcha!"

"Hi, Choy," Fagin said. "You're looking great."

"Still ready for ring, Fagin," Choy said, standing aside to admit him into the apartment. From a wealthy Chinese family, he had incurred his father's displeasure during the time he'd been a champion kick-boxer. Eventually, as a dutiful son, he had abandoned the sport to continue his education. "Donegan in bathroom. Make shit, shower, and shave."

"I'll wait," Fagin said, taking a seat on the battered sofa. "Where the hell is McKeever?"

"He go already." He gestured at the boxes stacked against the wall. "We move pretty damn quick. I don't tell you on the phone. No can talk about it. New assignment. New station."

Fagin frowned a bit in worry. "Where are you

going? Not out of country I hope."

"No. Go to coast. Place called Hai-Cat. That why we got seaplane, Fagin. Go on land. Go on water."

The sound of a toilet flushing could be heard from the nearby bathroom.

"Shit finish," Choy said. "Now shower and shave."

Fagin leaned toward the sound. "Hurry up, Donegan!"

The man's voice, muffled by the door, answered, "That you, Fagin? Choy said you called."

"Yeah, I want to talk to you. Can you go on an assignment?"

"No sweat," came the reply. "We're between jobs right now. Hang on, I'll be out in a jiffy."

"Hey, Fagin," Choy said. "You want a stout?"

"Sure," Fagin answered. "Ain't you packed your refrigerator yet?"

"Last thing," Choy said. "We keep plenty of suds — you betcha." He went into the kitchen and came out with a cold bottle of Guiness Stout.

"Ah!" Fagin said in appreciation. "Straight from Ireland, hey?"

"You betcha," Choy said. He laughed. "Donegan and McKeever say that if I drink one more case I turn into Irishman."

"That's right," Fagin answered with a grin. "I can remember when those two guys were Chinese. They drank so much of this stuff, they suddenly were zapped pure Irish."

"No shit?"

"No shit."

They were interrupted when Tim Donegan walked out of the bathroom. He was casually dressed in nothing but shorts and sandals. He greeted the visitor with a curt, "What's this about an assignment, Fagin?"

"I got some work for you," Fagin said.

"Yeah? Official stuff?"

"Not exactly," Fagin answered. "But I've got the funds to finance it." He took a sip of the stout. "By the way, what's this seaplane that Choy keeps talking about?"

"It's a Catalina PBY," Donegan answered. "An amphibious job."

Tim Donegan, Chief Petty Officer Retired, United States Navy, had been one of the last enlisted pilots remaining on the rosters when he finally left the service after twenty-five years as an airdale. Now a CIA pilot, he'd been flying for Air America in Southeast Asia for the previous two years. A slim man with thinning brown-gray hair, his craggy face seemed more like that of a saltwater sailor than a skilled pilot.

"I've got a job that involves a supply drop in Laos," Fagin said.

"What part?" Donegan asked. He walked toward the kitchen. "You want a stout, Choy?"

"Hell, no! I don't want to be no Irishman!"

"Okay. I'll bring you a can of dog food and you'll turn into a cocker spaniel, you silly shit," Donegan said. He came back with two stouts, giving one to the grinning Choy. "Where'd you say we were going in Laos?"

"The Cammon Plateau," Fagin answered.

Donnegan emitted a low whistle. "That's a tough place. Who's out there?"

"The Black Eagles."

"Jesus! Ain't they dead yet?" Donegan asked.

"They will be if we don't pull this off," Fagin said.

Donegan downed half the bottle. "In other words, we could be in deep shit ourselves, huh?"

"It's gonna be hairy as hell, Donegan. I won't lie to you," Fagin warned him.

Donegan ignored the warning. "First thing is to figure how we're gonna rig the aircraft for the operation. "I've only flown her once. The last serious work she done was patrol duty during World War II."

"Choy said you have a new assignment at Hai-Cat," Fagin remarked.

"Yeah. The place is an old French army R&R center. It's really nice. Right on a beach. We're finally getting a good berth," Donegan said. "After all those jungle hell-hole air strips, this is like a paradise." He finished the Guinness and tossed it into the corner where the bottle landed on a pile of similar containers. "When does this operation go down?"

"This minute," Fagin said. "I've drawn the supplies and have them loaded for a flight. I just had to find out where to have the goods delivered."

"Now you know," Donegan said. "Some movers are coming to pick up our shit here. Then we can leave for Hai-Cat."

"How soon will you be ready to leave?" Fagin asked.

"Early this afternoon, I guess," Donegan answered. "No later than six bells on the afternoon watch."

"I don't know that seafaring talk," Fagin complained. "What time?"

"Fifteen hundred hours—3 P.M."

"We drive over in my car," Choy said. "Take maybe two hours."

"Okay," Fagin said, standing up. "I'll go with you. Will there be room for my suitcase?"

"We'll make room," Donegan answered.

"You betcha!" Choy added.

"I'll have the stuff I've got for the resupply sent on the way," Fagin said. "It should be there when we arrive."

"By God, you are in a hurry, ain't you?" Donegan

said.

Fagin, walking back to the door, summed it up saying, "The lives of good men depend on it."

The afternoon shadows slowly grew longer as the Black Eagles crouched in the ravine. All ears strained for the sound of aircraft engines, but only the birds made noises in the sky.

Falconi, squatting down, consumed a can of C-ration pears. "The longer we sit here, the more chance there is of us getting spotted."

"Tell me about it," Archie said in agreement. "Are you sure this is the right day?"

"Yes. And the right place," Falconi said. "I've done three goddamned resections with map and compass. This—," he stamped the ground with his boot, "—is the exact spot on God's green earth where this detachment is supposed to be in order to receive the scheduled resupply parachute drop."

"I'm getting nervous," Archie said. He carefully crawled to the top of ravine, slowing raising his head to take a look around. "Shit!"

Falconi looked up as the detachment scout slid back to the floor of the gully. "What's the matter?"

"There's a cloud of dust showing on the eastern horizon," Archie said. "Vehicles of somes sort. It sure as hell ain't men."

Falconi picked up his radio. "Alpha. Bravo. This is Falcon. Vehicles coming into area. Stay low and quiet. Out."

Every Black Eagle crouched in the natural ditch, ears strained for a sound—any sound. But particularly one they yearned for—the distant whine of airplane engines.

After an hour, the faraway dull buzz of engines

could be heard. Top Gordon ended all speculation with a radio call to Falconi. "Falcon, this is Bravo. That noise is V12 diesel engines. Over."

Falconi made an immediate reply. "How can you be sure of the type? Over."

"Because," came back Top's broadcast, "I heard that type motor plenty in Korea. Them's Russian tanks. Out."

"Yeah," Archie said, again peering over the top of the ravine. "And the sonofabitches are coming this way!"

CHAPTER 9

Hai-Cat, located on the southern tip of South Viet Nam, was a former camp where, years previously, combat-weary French officers rested up between battles against the Viet-Minh. An excellent restaurant, several first-class bistros, and a bordello filled with beautiful whores were available for the rankers' enjoyment.

Now a CIA installation, some of the attractions had deteriorated, but it was still an ideal spot. A few quaint villages were located nearby that helped add character to the placid countryside that seemed to be out of reach of the shooting war.

A central administrative building dominated the scene. Small but comfortable bungalows—some air-conditioned—were scattered around the larger edifice. Walkways led to these quarters located among a few palm trees. It was a pleasant location where sea breezes wafted through the trees, lowering the temperature perceptively.

Down from the bungalows the tree line abruptly ended. Here a white, sandy beach stretched down to the blue China Sea. A breakwater of boulders had been constructed a scant fifty meters beyond the surf line, causing a man-made lagoon to form. A dock jutted out into the calm waters. Numerous transient boats, both military and civilian models used for intelligence purposes, were tied up at the pier. A large twin-engine seaplane was also moored on one side, bobbing in the gentle swells.

This was the near-luxurious destination of the car trip undertaken by Chuck Fagin, Mike Donegan, and Choy. They were given a close scrutiny at the gate by a trio of humorless, no-nonsense American military police. Showing ID cards wasn't enough for the three MPs. Positive identification and permission to enter Hai-Cat was not granted until a CIA officer came down from the administrative building to personally okay the applicants for entry. This man, a dour individual named Scott, as an old Southeast Asia area sweat, was closely acquainted with all three. But he had particular interest in Fagin.

"We got a transfer of funds down from Peterson Field," Scott said. "What the hell's going down?"

"It involves a group in Laos," Fagin answered.

"What program is ramrodding the operation?" Scott wanted to know.

Tim Donegan interjected, "Yeah. I was wondering about that too."

Fagin didn't want to have to explain the money he'd gotten from Taggart, or the fact that the whole thing was a scheme he'd hatched up himself. "Sorry, guys. The mission is classified as a Need-To-Know. It requires a special briefing."

Scott knew enough not to pry. "Sure, Fagin. Just thought it involved some folks I might know. I'm always anxious to hear news from some of my old buddies."

"I can tell you that the Black Eagles are in the middle of things," Fagin said.

"Don't tell me that crazy bastard Falconi and his

bandits are still alive!" Scott exclaimed.

Tim Donegan grinned. "That's what I said."

"Well, the sons of bitches are alive and kicking," Fagin said. "I got the logistical aspect of the operation plopped down in my lap. The first guy I thought of was my ol' pal Timothy Donegan."

Choy felt left out. "Hey! What about me?"

Fagin smiled and put his hand on the tough little Chinese guy's beefy shoulders. "Choy, I thought of you before I did Donegan. You're the best navigator in Air American. I just didn't want him to know about it."

"Yes," Choy said. "He is most sensitive."

"You two want to bullshit each other the rest of the day or go on down to our billets?" Donegan asked.

"McKeever is down at your plane," Scott said. "He's been tuning the goddamned engines all morning. We're all sick and tired of hearing them."

"Great," Donegan said. "Let's stash our gear, then go see how the plane is shaping up."

The three new arrivals climbed back into Choy's car. The Chinese airman drove through the gate down to the bungalow that Scott had told them was their new quarters. Fagin wanted to take a break and have a drink, but the two flying men were anxious to get down to take another look at their plane and to talk to their mechanic McKeever.

Mike McKeever, like Tim Donegan, was a retired sailor. Unlike Donegan, however, McKeever was never able to hold rank for any respectable length of time. The highest rate he earned in the navy was aviation machinist mate second class, though he'd tried to pass the test for first class petty officer no less than seven times in his bids for a rise in the enlisted men's hierarchy. Between a short attention span and a shorter temper, his conduct rating was not the highest in the United States Navy.

He was not exactly dumb, but sometimes he had a hell of a tough time reading things and expressing himself. That's why he liked engines. Once he was inside one, it seemed to sing out to him, telling the mechanic all its innermost secrets and problems. He liked the motors and the motors liked him.

McKeever was a hell of a big man. Six-feet-four and topping out at two-hundred and forty pounds, he carried a paunch built up over the years from consuming enough beer to be measured in metric tons. A rough-looking man, his large hands seemed to be perpetually stained with engine grease. Rarely smiling, he glared out at the world through pale-blue eyes. He kept his blond hair cut short to his large skull, but neglected to run a razor around his face for three or four days in a row.

Sitting on top of the plane's wing, he watched Fagin, Donegan, and McKeever walk down the dock toward him. "Hey!" McKeever yelled. "Did you bring any Guinness wit' you?"

Donegan stopped in his tracks. "You son of a bitch! Did you drink all the stuff we shipped down?"

"Hell, yes!" McKeever said indignantly. "They was on'y four cases and that was a little more'n a week ago."

"Hi ya, McKeever," Fagin called up to the big man.

"Hi ya, Fagin," McKeever yelled down. "Did ya brung any Guinness wit' you?"

"I prefer whiskey—Irish whiskey," Fagin answered.

"I don't like whiskey," McKeever said, crawling down from the wing. He walked across the nose of the big airplane, skipped over the front gun turret and dropped to the dock. The whole structure shook like an earthquake had struck it. "Whiskey is bad for Irishers."

"How do you figure that?" Fagin asked.

"God invented it so's we couldn't rule the world," McKeever said. "Tha's why I drink Guinness Stout."

"Aw, stop bellyaching," Donegan said. "We got some with us. We put it in the fridge." He pointed to the aircraft. "How's she shape up?"

"That there PBY is in A-number-one shape," McKeever said. "Them engines is purring like a coupla puppy dawgs."

Choy laughed. "Dogs no purr. Cats purr. Dogs bark." He punctuated his remark by imitating a hound. "Arf! Arf! Arf!"

"Then that plane be barkin' smooth," McKeever said. "Ruff! Ruff!"

Fagin winced. "I can't believe I'm going on a dangerous mission behind enemy lines with you screwballs."

McKeever's eyes lit up. "An operation? That's great, Fagin. I was getting bored and monotonized. We ain't did doodley shit for a long time."

Fagin looked past him at the airplane. "That is a beautiful flying machine."

"Amen!" Donegan added sincerely and almost reverently.

The aircraft they referred to was a PBY-5A Amphibian. Complete with gun stations—waist, nose, and a rather strange one called a "tunnel" that fired rearward and downward from a position under the tail—she carried bomb racks and was powered by a pair of Pratt and Whitney R-1830-92 engines that generated 1,200 horsepower. These had just been given a loving tuning up and check out by Mike McKeever.

With retractable landing gear, she was as much at home on water as on a runway. Her service ceiling was 16,200 feet and she could get up to a maximum of 178 miles an hour at 7,000 feet. In short, she was old but still strong and useful.

Particularly with a crew that would love and respect her.

Fagin sat around thirsty and irritated while the crew gave their airship an affectionate inspection. McKeever proudly insisted that they listen to the engines he'd spent so much time tuning. Tim Donegan went through no less than three complete pilot checklists to get what feel of the airplane he could even though it was moored at the dock.

Choy, a licensed, experienced navigator who had flown as third officer on Taiwanese airliners, carefully checked out his own stations, noting the radios and navigation equipment. He did his job either in the co-pilot's seat, the bow compartment, or at the radio/navigation station behind the cockpit.

Fagin groaned and complained, but there was nothing he could do to hurry the three airmen up. Finally, in late afternoon, they were satisfied and left the dock to return to their bungalow.

A couple of hours later, the evening breezes off the ocean flowed gently through the bungalow that had been assigned to Donovan, McKeever, and Choy. They and their visitor Chuck Fagin had enjoyed a good western meal of steak and fries at the cafeteria located in the administration building. Now, their stomachs stuffed with the meat and potatoes, they sat around the living room sipping on Guinness Stouts. A special order of the brew had arrived that same afternoon.

Although Fagin didn't mind the stout, he had other preferences. "Don't you guys ever drink anything else?"

Donegan shrugged. "What else is there?"

"Oh," Fagin mused, "there's whiskey, gin, vodka—"

"All we ask out of life is decent chow, a good plane to fly, and plenty of Guinness Stout," Donegan said. "The stuff is great and it's from the land of our ancestors."

"You betcha!" Choy interjected.

Fagin frowned. "What the hell does that have to do with you?"

"These two bastards make me honorary Irishman," Choy said. "Anyhow you say if I drink enough Guinness I turn into Irishman."

"Yeah," Donovan said. "And if you eat enough shit you'll turn into a turd."

"If I eat shit I get sick," Choy said seriously.

McKeever, never one for much conversation, wanted to get down to brass tacks. "What's this here mission you want for us to fly, Fagin?"

"I've explained that it's to the Black Eagles," Fagin said. "A supply drop in Laos."

"What do they be doing in Laos?" McKeever wanted to know. "Anyhow I figgered them crazy bastards dead a long time ago."

"Well they ain't, and I can't tell you what they're doing because it's a Need-To-Know situation," Falconi intoned. Those three words—most powerful in the intelligence community—meant that unless an individual's job required certain knowledge, he wasn't going to get it. The mere sound or sight of "Need-To-Know" cut off all argument with its connotation of required special briefings and limited access.

Choy, as the navigator of their crew, was more interested in location anyway. "What area of Laos, Fagin?"

Fagin smiled apologetically. "I'm not real sure."

Donegan's eyes opened wide. "Wait a minute! Are we talking about flying around the entire country of Laos looking for a bunch of crazy, unpredictable bastards like Falconi and his Black Eagles?"

"Not exactly *all* over Laos," Fagin said. "Just the Cammon Plateau."

"That narrows it down," Donegan said sarcastically. "We only got a few hundred thousand square miles to deal with." He looked straight at Fagin. "That don't make me feel any better. There's something here that don't jell, Fagin, and don't gimme that Need-To-Know shit now."

"Okay I'll level with you guys," Fagin said. "Falconi and his outfit have been left out in the cold on account of supplies and energies being aimed at a different part of the war."

McKeever nodded his understanding. "They were unprioritized, huh?"

Fagin frowned. "Where do you get those words?"

"I hear 'em," McKeever said.

Choy laughed. "You hear words then turn around."

The big Irish air mechanic sneered. "You just think you're hot shit on account of you can talk Chinese."

"I hot shit, you betcha!"

"Go on, Fagin," McKeever said impatiently.

"There's not much else to say," Fagin said. "The sponsoring agency had to turn their resources in another direction. Until they can get back to the original plan, Falconi is high and dry."

Donegan displayed an almost impish Irish grin. "Where'd you get the operating funds, Fagin?"

"Need-To-Know," Fagin replied.

Now McKeever laughed out loud. "You stole some money, din't you, Fagin?"

"No," Fagin said truthfully.

Donegan leaned forward. "We don't give a shit one way or the other. You've got the dough for the gas and our time, that's fine. I'll turn the chit into my bureau chief and he's happy."

"What about the stuff we're gonna drop?" McKeever asked.

"It's on the way now," Fagin said. "Small bundles of ammo, rations, and anti-tank rockets."

Now Donegan's mouth dropped open. "Is that insane character going up against tanks?" He guffawed, throwing his head back. "I gotta hand it to our ol' pal Falconi! If they gave him an OPORD to attack Moscow at high noon during the May Day celebration, he'd do it."

McKeever, who's sense of humor matched his intellect, asked, "How we gonna get the stuff out the airplane?"

Fagin looked at Donegan. "There's a problem?"

"This ain't a cargo aircraft, Fagin," the pilot explained. "It's designed for patrolling and some light bombing." He was thoughtful for a few minutes. "Did you say they're small bundles?"

"Yeah," Fagin said. "No more than a yard square."

"Hell, we'll throw 'em out the side blisters," Donegan said.

"That'll be fun," McKeever said.

Choy the navigator had a problem. "How we find Falconi, huh? I can map a course to take us anyplace you want. But I got to know where to go."

"I figure we can fly straight over the Cammon Plateau, then try to raise Falconi by radio and when we do, we'll make arrangements to get the goods to him."

"Why don't we contact him from here?" Donegan asked. "There's a powerful transmitter aboard this here station."

"Falconi hasn't got anything big to receive or broadcast with," Fagin said. "Only Prick-Six radios. We'll have to fly close so we can talk to him from the plane."

"Then that's all we can do," Donegan said. He finished his Guinness, then got up and went into the kitchen, bringing back four more for his companions. He passed the bottles around, then sat down. Peering thoughtfully out the bungalow window, he said, "It'll be dark in another hour."

"Yeah," McKeever said.

Choy got one of the fresh stouts. "Does Falconi know he is forgotten man?"

"He does now," Fagin said. "His first drop was due early this afternoon."

Donegan shook his head. "I'll bet he's really pissed off."

Fagin nodded. "I wonder what Falconi and his guys are doing right now."

CHAPTER 10

The sun was low in the sky but as far as Lieutenant Colonel Robert Falconi and his Black Eagles were concerned, there was still too much daytime left.

"C'mon, sunset," Archie Dobbs said with an urgent tone in his voice. "Time is dragging too much."

"You're just wishing your life away," Falconi, standing nearby, remarked.

"No, sir," he countered. "I'm wishing that Russki armor away."

The Russian Tanks were not traveling parallel with or away from the Detachment. The steel monsters were rolling slowly and steadily toward them.

Archie, his head barely above the ravine, studied the approaching T-55s in his binoculars. "I wonder if they know we're here," he mused aloud.

Falconi, standing below him, shook his head. "I doubt it. But they're looking for us."

"Yeah," Archie agreed. "They're prob'ly really pissed off about us doing in them other tanks, huh?"

"Yeah," Falconi said. "I'd say the incident didn't exactly give them cause to throw a party." He raised his team leaders on the radio. "Alpha, Bravo, this is Falcon. Get your rocketeers primed and ready. From the looks of things, those armored vehicles are trying to locate us. Out."

Both teams broke into activity making sure that the extra LAWS were all within reach of either Gunnar Olson or Steve Matsuno. When that was done, the Black Eagles settled down to more of the nerve-wracking waiting.

"Remember," Falconi cautioned Archie. "No more heroics. Let Steve and Gunnar take care of those tanks."

Archie nodded. "Yes, sir." He grinned weakly. "To tell you the truth, I ain't in the mood to run out there again."

In only twenty minutes it was obvious something had to be done. The Detachment had no place to go. If they stayed in the ravine, the Tanks would eventually roll right up to them. On the other hand, in the event the Black Eagles tried to pull a withdrawal, they would be quickly spotted.

Archie, still manning his observation post, looked down at his commanding officer. "Sir, I think it's safe to assume that the shit is about to hit the fan, right?"

Falconi didn't answer. Instead he hit the transmit button on his radio. "Alpha, Bravo, this is Falcon. Prepare your rocketeers to fire on my order. Also detail one extra man to handle a LAWS. Out."

Ray Swift Elk and Top Gordon went to work in their respective squads. Several LAWS were put within easy reach of Steve Matsuno and Gunnar Olson. Blue Richards in the Alpha Team and Loco Padilla in the Bravo, were assigned to augment the regular rocketeers.

Falconi pulled Archie down from his perch and took his place. He started to use his binoculars, but the T-55s were so close it wasn't necessary. He counted six of them. Speaking loudly, he said, "Archie, fetch me a LAWS from Gunnar."

"You ain't gonna try to be a hero, are you?" Archie asked.

"Knock off the wisecracks and grab me a LAWS!"

"Coming up, sir!"

Archie rushed down the ravine to the Alphas' position. He grabbed one of the disposable rockets.

"Hey, Archie!" Lieutenant Ray Swift Elk yelled. "Falconi told you not to try any more shit."

"I ain't, sir, honest. The Old Man wants it for hisself." He quickly returned, passing the weapon up to Falconi.

The lieutenant colonel, watching the approaching armored unit, grimaced. "Those are awful looking sons of bitches when they're coming at you."

"Yes, sir," Archie agreed.

Falconi flipped up the sight and aimed it dead on the leading battle wagon. After taking a deep breath and holding it, he slowly pressed down on the firing boot.

The rocket ignited, flying out of the tube in a straight trajectory. It hit the tank tread just below the left mud shield. The explosion blew off the idling wheel and split the tread, causing the T-55 to swerve crazily then come to an abrupt stop.

At almost that exact moment, Steve Matsuno cut loose with his own LAWS. His target had turned toward its damaged partner, leaving its bazooka plate exposed. Steve's rocket slammed into the heavy steel plate, but hit at a glancing angle. The resulting explosion bent that portion of the vehicle a bit, but did not disable the tank.

Gunnar Olson, meanwhile, was having a hell of a time getting a good sight picture on any of the other rolling monsters. They were behind the first two, wisely scuttling back and forth as their angry gunners sought a target to fire their cannon and machine guns at.

With the second armored vehicle still roaring toward him, Steve Matsuno yelled over at Blue Richards. "Go for the sonofabitch, Blue!"

Blue, on old coon hunter, went for the spot where the cannon barrel joined the turret. He fired, able to see the projectile streak true and straight. It exploded, most of the force of the detonation going off into thin air.

But it did useful damage.

The tube of the 100-millimeter gun was thrown out of alignment. But from the way the turret pivoted toward the Alpha Team, it was obvious the tank crew didn't know about the disabled cannon. Their machine gun set up a chatter and the breech-block of the weapon could be heard slamming shut. The unfortunate gunner inside the T-55 jerked the firing mechanism. The charges inside the casing exploded true, but the shell only made it half way down the ruined tube.

All the gases blew back inside the tank.

With smoke pouring from its armored viewing hatches, the big battle wagon went into a lazy turn, its crew inside dead from a combination of blast and concussion.

The tank, rolling slowly out of the formation, left its friends in the rear exposed for Gunnar Olson. The stoic Norwegian-American took careful aim and blasted straight at the nearest T-55. The rocket hit true, burning itself inside the tank in a millisecond during the resultant explosion.

Now it was Loco Padilla's turn. The marine, anxious to make a kill, crawled out of the ravine. Jumping up, he ran toward a shallow depression in the ground, diving into it. He quickly prepared the LAWS for a launch as the nearest armored vehicle rolled relentlessly and steadily toward him.

Malpractice McCorkel, watching him, yelled a warning. "Fire at the bastard, Loco. For the love of God! He's closing in fast on you."

Loco raised the sight and raised the tube to fire. The big tank had closed it faster than he expected. He then realized that if he hit the T-55, the explosion would get him too.

Top Gordon, the only Black Eagle experienced in fighting against tanks, knew what had happened. "The big bastards roar down on you faster than you expect. They're a hundred meters away, then in a second or two they're right on top of you."

Gunnar Olson, watching in horrid fascination, was tempted to fire but knew it would be useless. His own rocket would be as deadly to Loco as to the tank. "What the fuck's he gonna do?"

"The right thing," Top said. "Look! He's ducking!"

Loco pressed himself down into the dirt of the dent in the ground. The battle wagon rolled over him.

"Shit!" Gunnar yelled. "He's squashed!"

"No he ain't!" Malpractice exclaimed. "Look!"

The tank had passed over the brave marine without touching him. Now Loco sat up. He waited for the T-55 to get a few more meters away as he again took aim. This time he fired.

The rocket slammed into the turret bustle, blowing down through the engine louvers. Another loud explosion sounded from the interior as the initial hit did internal damage. It was so powerful the big tank jumped off the ground.

Now Loco got up and ran like hell back toward the ravine. Machine gun fire from one of the surviving armored vehicles splattered around him. He hit the ground and rolled over the edge of the gully, falling heavily to the bottom.

Malpractice ran up to him, ready to perform his duties as detachment medic. "You okay, Loco?"

Breathing heavily, the marine grinned. "Yeah—I got—pissed off—at them—bastards—"

Sergeant Major Top Gordon spoke with respect in his voice. "You are one crazy sonofabitch!"

"That's why—they call me—Loco," he said. "In Spanish it means—"

"I know! I know!" Top interrupted. "It means 'Crazy'."

Gunnar's full attention was directed at the nearest tank. Ky Luyen tapped him on the shoulder. "Look at other one, Gunnar. Bad shit going down. See?"

Gunnar switched his steady gaze over to the T-55 charging toward the Alphas. Both machine guns were spitting flame and slugs, the fusillades kicking up dust along the top of the ravine. Gunnar glanced back at his own tank. He made a quick decision, firing at the one threatening the Alphas.

The rocket hit, but not true, leaving only a wide scorch mark along the mantelet. Ky yelled, "Shoot him again, Gunnar. I take the other!"

Gunnar, not remembering that Ky had no LAWS, complied by preparing another LAWS.

Meanwhile, Ky leaped up and raced in a crouch at an angle that kept him from the tank crew's view. Then he abruptly turned inward toward the rear of the other battle wagon. He managed to reach it, grabbing the field telephone on the outside. This device was used for communication with the vehicle's interior by infantry troops.

"Chao ong!" Ky screamed in Vietnamese. *"Toi la ban!* We are comrades. This is a big mistake!"

The T-55 halted as Ky spoke fast and furious demanding to know why the tanks had attacked. A brief exchange with the armored vehicle commander followed, but it was interrupted by a loud explosion as the tank that had caught Gunnar's attention was blown to hell by his LAWS.

Now Ky scrambled aboard the vehicle, still yelling into the telephone. He banged on the turret hatch with his rifle, playing the role of a man who had been fired on by his own troops. Now, as he spoke, he pulled a grenade from his patrol harness.

The hatch opened halfway. *"Ai do?"* came a voice from the T-55's interior.

Ky quickly shoved the grenade through the small opening and leaped off the vehicle. The sound of cursing in Vietnamese was followed by the detonation of the grenade.

There was no more movement from the tank.

The Black Eagles emitted a spontaneous cheer. Clambering out of the ravine, they looked at the smoking hulks of armor. Gunnar Olson, however, wasn't smiling. He pushed his way through the others until he reached Steve Matsuno. "How many LAWS do you guys have left?"

"None," Steve said. "They're all gone now."

"So are ours," Gunnar said.

"Well, buddy," Steve said. "As they say in California, 'We're in deep yogurt now'!"

The four Russians sat under the thatched roof of the screened-in hut and perspired.

They sweated bucketfuls as the salty liquid oozed from their pores, seeping through the khaki denim of their summer uniforms, soaking them as if they'd been sitting beneath a spray of luke warm water. Even their broad-brimmed summer field hats drooped from the effects of the heat.

These men were a full crew of their own T-55 tank.

They were Captain Anatole Krushenko, tank commander; Senior Lieutenant Konstantin Bulovich, gunner; Lieutenant Dimitri Pavlov, driver; and Junior Lieutenant Pavel Brigis, loader.

The reason for this unusually high rank for a single tank crew was because they were stationed in Laos as armored force instructors to the North Vietnamese Army operating in the area. Their duty required not only classroom work, but plenty of practical work in turning soldiers who were former primitive rice-planting farmers into modern tankers operating state-of-the art battle tanks.

Only recently assigned to the job, the steamy weather of Southeast Asia pressed down on the cold-weather soldiers like a suffocating blanket. The Russians, from a land of long, frigid winter nights and only short mild summers, were physically and psychologically unprepared for the strength-sapping climate of that part of the world.

Bulovich raised his glass of vodka. *"Za vasheh zdavrovyeh!"* he said sarcastically.

Krushenko, the leader, smiled sardonically. He downed his own glass of the potent liquor. "This is the only thing that is keeping me going, comrades."

The lieutenant named Brigis was not really a Russian. He hailed from Latvia, but he graduated with distinction from the Armored Force Academy and earned a good posting in the Soviet Army. He laughed at the sardonic humor. "In all my days at cadet school, I never thought I would be riding around Indo-China in a T-55 with a drunken crew."

"Ha!" exclaimed Pavlov. "You are always the drunkest."

"Where do you think I get my courage to go with you crazy *vnebrayin?*"

"Let me propose another toast," Krushenko said.

"To our beloved Mother Russia. May we see her again soon."

"Da!" the others exclaimed in unison. *"Mat Rosiya!"*

They downed the vodka. Once again the bottle was passed around and the glasses refilled. Bulovich got drunkenly to his feet and was about to offer another toast when their North Vietnamese translator appeared. He was a worrisome captain named Chin Hoa. "Excuse me, comrades," the NVA officer said.

Krushenko, his eyes half closed, turned and glared at the man. "Now what, Comrade Chin Hoa? Are you here to tell us that the North Vietnamese meteorological bureau is reporting that tomorrow the weather is turning hot.

Drunken laughter followed the sarcasm.

But Chin Hoa's face was sober. "We have lost more tanks, Comrades. Six of them."

Bulovich almost sobered up from the bad news. He jumped to his feet. "How can this be? We have trained the North Vietnamese comrades for many weeks."

Brigis shook his head. "But who is destroying these tanks? Who can it be?"

"The last radio transmission from the final tank that was destroyed reported the situation in full," Chin Hoa said. "The tank commander spoke most lucidly. The enemy fired rockets and were easily seen to be Occidentals. The comrade heard words shouted in English."

"Amerikanski?" Pavlov asked. "How could such a thing happen. I didn't know they had active units in Laos!"

Krushenko was now sober. "Of course. They have finally heard of the North Vietnamese tank unit in this area. They have surmised what its mission is. An anti-armor unit has been sent to defeat them."

"What are we to do?" Bulovich asked. "The North Vietnamese are not ready to take on such opposition. They will be wiped out piecemeal."

"I will answer your question in a simple direct manner," Krushenko said. "We will personally lead the comrades in a counter-attack against the invaders."

"They will find it different when they face a crew of Russian experts," Pavlov said, pouring himself another drink. "We were weaned on petrol and raised on cold steel."

Krushenko reached over and took the glass away from his fellow officer. "No more drinking, Comrade Senior Lieutenant. Killing Americans is work for sober men."

CHAPTER 11

Archie Dobbs' eyes were red-rimmed with fatigue. His feet dragged and he moved almost lethargically across the flat terrain of the Cammon Plateau. In spite of his near exhaustion, his nerves kept him on the alert and the awful tiredness did nothing to diminish his amazing sense of direction.

Lieutenant Colonel Robert Falconi's orders had been explicit that previous evening after knocking out the half dozen tanks:

"We're going to get the hell out of here before those bastards' buddies show up looking for us," the Black Eagle commander had announced to the Detachment. "Trying to deal with tanks armed only with M16s and a couple of 203s would be like taking on a herd of buffalo with peashooters."

"Are we pulling out of the mission?" Archie had asked.

"Hell no!" Falconi snapped. "I've never signed a Quit Slip in my life and I'm not starting now." He calmed down a bit, winking at his scout. "I've just got to have some time to figure out how to kill a buffalo with a peashooter."

The result of Falconi's decision for a strategic withdrawal was a long night-long march without breaks.

There was no choice in the matter. Any more enemy troops showing up would be sounding the trumpets of doom for the Black Eagles. The Order of the Day was to put as much distance as possible between the battle site and themselves in the shortest amount of time.

The moon was bright with only a few clouds to obscure its light. This forced Archie to move along ravines and creeks to take advantage of the shadows they cast. This slowed their journey considerably, but only when it was absolutely necessary did the scout take off on a cross-country trek. And he kept the time of exposure down to the bare minimum.

Now, out over the far eastern horizon, a pink glow barely showed. The approaching dawn heralded the end of the Black Eagles' eighth continual hour of steady movement. Archie almost breathed a sigh of relief when Falconi's voice broke over the receiver of his radio.

"Scout, this is Falconi. Find a good place to hole up for the day. Over."

"Roger, Falcon," Archie answered. "I see a creek about fifty meters ahead. Does that sound okay? Over."

"Roger. We'll grab some camouflage there," Falconi said. "Move out. Over."

"You mean we ain't gonna stay there? Over," Archie asked.

"Negative, goddamnit!" came back Falconi's reply. "That's just the kind of terrain feature where the sons of bitches will be looking for us. Out."

Archie increased the pace as the sun's light grew perceptively brighter. When they reached the creek, Falconi ordered everyone to take machete in hand and cut some brush for cover.

Top Gordon, always the undiplomatic and pragmatic senior non-commissioned officer, growled,

"Don't take it all out of one area and leave unnatural gaps in the goddamned bushes! We don't want 'em to know we been here. Spread out and take a little here and a little there."

The men, working quickly, obeyed. Within fifteen minutes all had enough branches to cover themselves. After being careful to leave no tracks in or around the area, they moved out again. This time they went only two hundred meters until they reached an elongated basin in the ground. This depression was deep enough to hide them from view at a distance, but not enough to afford them any protection from incoming fire.

"Okay," Falconi ordered. "Make some low hootches with your ponchos and cover 'em. And don't get too comfortable. Keep your boots on and equipment ready to haul ass in an instant. We'll be on fifty percent alert all day, so let's keep the teams together."

Once more the men turned to the assigned task, and—as he'd done before—Top checked everything out. He corrected the way Gunnar piled up too much of the cut branches on one end of his poncho. Then he made Loco Padilla rearrange his when he thought it looked too phony. By the time Top finished, the area looked like it was a small stand of small, innocent bushes that had been growing naturally in the basin for years.

The last thing the sergeant major did was pick out half the men to stand the first guard, then he ordered the others into their camouflaged hootches for some badly needed sleep.

Thus, threatened by heavy armor, unsupported, and far from home, the Black Eagles settled down for a few hours of quiet—they hoped—rest.

* * *

Tim Donegan eased the throttles of the two Pratt & Whitney engines forward. He listened in satisfaction as the synchronized sound of the blasting engines stayed in tune with each other.

"Mike did number one job," Choy said from the copilot's seat. As an experienced navigator and flier, he could well appreciate the sound of finely tuned power plants.

The big PBY eased forward away from the dock, then gradually picked up speed as the propeller pitch changed with the increase in throttle pressure. The aircraft skipped a bit across the water. Chuck Fagin, seated in the radio/navigator's compartment with Mike McKeever, glanced out the hatch on the port side. "She's kinda slow lifting off, isn't she?"

McKeever nodded. "Yeah. The water is smooth close to the dock and makes a suction. When we get farther out where it's more choppy she'll fly alright. You can bet your ass on that."

Fagin wasn't amused. "Hey, pal, I *am* betting my ass on it. And the Black Eagles', too!"

A few moments passed, then McKeever's prediction came true. The rougher water broke the fuselage loose from the ocean surface. The aircraft lifted slowly, then climbed faster. Once they were really airborne, Fagin undid his safety belt and opened the door leading to the cockpit. He stepped through, standing behind Donegan and Choy.

"How's she look?"

Donegan was grinning happily. "Beautiful! This is one hell of an airplane." He glanced over at Choy. "Have you worked out a course for us, or have you been sitting there with your thumbs up you ass."

"You shithead!" Choy said happily. "I work out course last night. Go to zero-zero-four."

"Zero-zero-four," Donegan said. "Roger." He eased

the PBY on course. "How soon will we be there?"

Although Choy didn't have much of a facility when it came to learning languages, he was a mathematical whiz with a good education. A slide rule was evident in the side pocket of his flight suit. "You cruise at one-hundred fifty knots. We be over Cammon Plateau in one hour, five minutes. You betcha!"

Now Mike McKeever joined them. "I got that Browning .50 mounted in the nose. Notice any difference?"

Donegan, having to work the controls manually because of no auto-pilot, shook his head. "Nope. She's flying smooth as can be. The machine gun's weight hasn't caused any aerodynamic affects that I can notice. You done a good job, ol' buddy."

"I'm a good mechanic," McKeever stated matter-of-factly.

"You know your shit," Choy added.

"Hey, I'm impressed!" Fagin said. "A big old Browning, huh? All you need is some bombs."

"Looky, Fagin," McKeever said, grabbing the CIA officer's shoulder. "See that thing between the struts and the floats?"

"Yeah," Fagin answered.

"That there's a bomb rack. There's one on each wing and they'll hold two bombs up to five hunnerd pounds. Whattaya think of 'at?"

"I think 'at is pretty impressive," Fagin said. He nudged Choy. "What about the radio?"

"All tuned up," Choy answered. "Turn her on and use her."

Fagin checked his watch. "It's too early, but once we're over the Cammon Plateau I'm going to start transmitting to raise Falconi."

Donegan, keeping his eyes on the instruments, leaned back to speak to Fagin. "Our radio is damned

112

good. But if them Black Eagles got nothing but Prick-Sixes we'll have to be right on top of 'em before they can pick up your broadcasts."

"It's all we can do," Fagin said.

Donegan nodded. "Yeah. If we—"

"Hey!" Choy interrupted him. "Keep the course zero-zero-four. You go to zero-zero-six you dumb shit! You want to go to Red China?"

Donegan sneered. "Remind me to throw you into the South China Sea when we can back over it."

"Hey!" Choy exclaimed. "Fuck you! I'm not gonna remind you of nothing like that."

"You guys," Fagin said, "are the craziest sons of bitches I've ever known outside Falconi and his bunch."

"You gotta be crazy to do this," Donegan said. "We're flying in a twenty-five-year-old airplane over enemy country hoping to find a small group of guys somewhere in an area of hundreds of thousands of square miles. And to top it off, the dumb bastards got little bitty shitty radios that ain't good for nothing but short-range patrols."

"It's damned difficult," Fagin admitted. "But in a war like this you've got to be bold and audacious. Only the most dedicated, unswerving, almost fanatical and dedicated individuals can perform difficult and near impossible feats."

"Anybody want a ham sandwich?" McKeever asked.

The Pathet Lao infantrymen were drawn up in four unswerving ranks. Wearing sandals, shorts, collarless shirts, Russian army web gear, and carrying AK47 rifles, these small men looked mean and determined.

Over to one side, wearing regular North Vietnamese uniforms supplemented with Soviet padded tanker helmets, NVA armor troops were also smartly drawn up. They stood in front of their three T-55 tanks.

The four Russian officers—Captain Krushenko, Senior Lieutenant Bulovich, Lieutenant Pavlov, and the Latvian Junior Lieutenant Brigis—were arranged on top of their own battle wagon.

The situation for them had deteriorated to a face-saving operation. Well trained in dealing with various Oriental troops in their own country, the quartet fully realized their prestige had slipped badly with the losses of the other tanks.

"Chao ong, Comrades," Krushenko said in Vietnamese. He paused while the official translator for the Pathet Lao riflemen put his words into their language. "Sad misfortunes have befallen our comrades. It is something we do not well understand. After teaching them the tactics of the great Soviet liberation army, we cannot understand how they could have been defeated. The only reason for such a catastrophe is, of course, that it was caused by overwhelming forces."

The Southeast Asian soldiers nodded in understanding as they listened to the words. After being filled with self-confidence and put through rigorous tank-infantry training, they had felt invincible.

"We may sit here and remain stunned and saddened by the martyrdom of the unfortunate comrades," Krushenko said. "Or, we can become angry and desire revenge."

An angry murmur sounded among the assembled Red troops.

Krushenko knew they were gearing up to go along with whatever mood he decided to put them in. "I say that we become furious in the name of World Socialism! I say that we mount an operation for vengeance!"

Now there were some shouts from the soldiers.

"My comrades and I are going to personally lead you into this battle!" Krushenko said. "Our own tank will be in the vanguard on a mission I have decided to call Operation Mest." He paused. "Does anyone here know what the Russian word *mest* means in your language?"

Naturally the Pathet Lao translator spoke up loudly. "It means 'vengeance', comrade!"

"Exactly," Krushenko said. He gave a subtle signal for the other Russians behind him to stand up. When they were poised, the captain shouted, "Pathet Lao infantrymen! Put yourselves into your skirmish formations as we have taught you! North Vietnamese tankers! Man your vehicles and maneuver into the proper attack positions on each side of our T-55. We will find the enemy this day and smash him. *Mau len! Toroplivost!"*

Now shouting, the Oriental soldiers quickly and excitedly obeyed the grimacing Russian.

Malpractice McCorkel sprawled in a relaxed prone position. Although he was tired from the previous night's march, he'd enjoyed two luxurious hours of sleep in his quickly constructed hootch before Top Gordon had nudged him awake.

"Guard duty, Malpractice," Top informed him.

"On my way, Top," Malpractice answered. Grabbing his rifle, he'd responded immediately. He went to the spot indicated by the sergeant major and plopped down beside Ky Luyen. "Okay, Ky. Take a nap."

"Good deal," Ky said, using a phrase he'd quickly

learned from his American comrades-in-arms. "The tireds have got me bad."

Malpractice grinned as the tough little guy moved off to catch some sleep. Then the medical sergeant had settled in to maintain an alert watch as did a half dozen other Black Eagles.

For the most part it was a boring chore. Heat waves danced across the distant horizon on the Cammon Plateau giving indication that there was plenty of nothing out there.

Then that changed.

Malpractice caught a glimmer of movement in the distant haze. At first he wasn't sure, but after another minute passed, the combat veteran was positive. He grabbed his binoculars and took a long careful look.

"Shit!" He spat. "Sergeant Major! Tanks and infantry to the north! And they're closing in fast!"

CHAPTER 12

Chuck Fagin sat in the radio operator's seat of the PBY amphibious airplane. The earphones clamped on his head were tight-fitting old World War II models. But he didn't notice the discomfort as he fiddled with the dial, making sure the old communications set was on the proper frequency. After a quick adjustment, he once again began his transmission.

"Falcon, this is Aircraft. Over. Falcon, this is Aircraft. Over."

Mike McKeever, sitting on the other side of the compartment, watched him through half-closed eyes. The big man stretched his long legs, which reached almost halfway across the deck. "That's monotonous, ain't it?"

"Yeah," Fagin answered after finishing another quick transmission.

"Don't your throat get sore?" McKeever asked.

"I'm a tough bastard," Fagin said.

"What about being bored? Ain't you bored?"

"I'm trying to do a job," Fagin said. "And unlike a lot of people around here, I've got an attention span that goes a bit beyond five or ten seconds."

McKeever, missing the point, shrugged. "So what? Don't it still get boring?"

Fagin looked around at the aircraft mechanic. "I do this a lot," he said. "And it ain't boring. The last time was from a submarine a hundred feet under the sea."

McKeever laughed. "Now you're doing radio talk up in the air. Next time you can do it on the ground, huh, Fagin? Or maybe you'll do it from a deep hole."

"If I don't raise Falconi on this radio, there ain't gonna be a next time," Fagin said. He turned back to his task. "Falcon, this is Aircraft. Over. Falcon, this is Aircraft. Over."

McKeever yawned and stretched. "That Falconi was bound and determined to get hisself killed one day. If he don't do it now, he'll do it later." He yawned again. "On the other hand he might have did it already."

"Thanks for the encouragement, McKeever," Fagin said angrily. "You're a kind man—the kind that oughta be run outta town."

McKeever smirked. "The joke's on you 'cause that's already been did to me, Fagin."

The CIA man hit the transmit button once again. "Falcon, this is Aircraft. Over. Falcon, this is Aircraft. Over."

The Black Eagles who had just come off guard duty had barely managed to slip into a deep sleep before they were rudely awakened. In spite of their fatigue, their senses jumped to a hundred percent state of alert when the sergeant major went from hootch to hootch waking them up.

"Open them baby blues! Bad guys closing in!"

Falconi, the first notified of the approaching enemy by the sergeant major, crawled up to the spot where Malpractice McCorkel studied the movement out on the plateau. The comanding officer joined the medical sergeant. "How's it look, Malpractice? Think we'll be up to our eyeballs in Pathet Lao and Russian tanks pretty soon?"

"Maybe. They're coming straight this way, sir," Malpractice said, not removing his binoculars from his eyes. "I can't figure out why. They couldn't know we're bivouacked on this exact spot. They might just be plain dumb lucky, sir."

Falconi glanced rearward, noticing a mountain peak barely showing in the distance. "They're attracted this way by a prominent terrain feature. It's a natural thing if a man's got no particular azimuth to follow or doesn't have a compass."

"Too bad we didn't notice that before we settled in here," Malpractice remarked. "But I guess it wasn't light enough."

"We'll just have to sit tight," Falconi said, now using his own field glasses. "Maybe they'll veer off in one direction or the other."

Now Malpractice lowered his binoculars. He glanced back at their impromptu camp. "We did a hell of a good job of camouflage, sir. They might just waltz right on by."

"Sure," Falconi said. "It's either that or stumble straight into us—tanks and all."

Captain Anatol Krushenko of the Soviet Army Armored Corps sat in the turret of the T-55 tank. The vehicle's hatches and ventilators were wide open, yet the interior of the battle wagon was like an oven. Krushenko could tell the difference in the temperature between where his head and shoulders were in the fresh outside air, and his body, which soaked up the heat from the inside bulkheads like a baking goose.

Finally Senior Lieutenant Konstantin Bulovich's strained voice sounded below the captain's feet from the gunner's position. "We've got to stop, Comrade Captain! Pavlov's face is turning beet red."

"*Proklinat!*" Krushenko cursed. But he slipped down to the tank's floor and leaned forward to examine the driver. "Let's have a look at you, Comrade Lieutenant."

Pavlov's face was almost bright scarlet. His breath was shallow and labored, but he tried to put on a show of bravado. "It's a bit warm. That's all."

"We will stop and get out of this blasted furnace," Krushenko said. "But listen to me. I do not want the North Vietnamese comrades to think we are suffering from the high temperature. We have already been embarrassed enough by having to take the blame for those incompetents who got themselves killed. They'll fault us for giving them poor training before they'll admit their pals' bonehead antics."

Brigis, licking his dry lips, offered a suggestion. "Why not act like we are studying the map?" He was soaking wet, reclining in the chair where the loader rode between combat actions. "Everybody knows the damned things are out of date anyhow."

"*Korozhi!*" Krushenko quickly returned to his position and radioed the North Vietnamese tank commanders. The entire convoy came to a halt. The Russians quickly climbed out of their T-55, gathering in the shade of the vehicle as Pavel Brigis produced a map from his coverall pockets. They feigned studying it while dragging their canteens out of the carriers.

"My water is almost gone," Bulovich complained. He glanced over at the North Vietnamese who lounged comfortably around their own tanks. "Look at those *keltie* monkeys! They are completely unaffected by this horrible weather."

"They were born here," Krushenko reminded him. "They know nothing of the cleansing, clear cold of winter."

"What beautiful words!" Bulovich said. A picture of a crisp, frigid day with fresh, white snow danced through the Russian's mind.

Pavlov weaved slightly on his feet. Although he'd recovered a bit after leaving the sweltering interior of the T-55, he was still wobbly. "We must get water, Comrade Captain. We have perspired so much that we are close to dehydration."

Bulovich still watched the North Vietnamese. "They are not even thirsty!"

Krushenko, studying the map, walked around the tank acting as if he were comparing some terrain feature with the chart. "There is what appears to be a creek a few kilometers away," he said. "We will go there." He turned and gestured to Pavlov. "See that faraway mountain?"

Pavlov squinted his eyes. *"Da, Tovarisch Kapitan."*

"Drive straight toward it," Krushenko instructed him. "That seems to be the shortest route to water."

Choy slipped through the hatchway leading to the navigator/radio operator's compartment. He gave the napping Mike McKeever only a cursory glance before squatting beside Fagin. "We run up and down here pretty good, Fagin. I think it time to move to another place."

"Have you guys seen anything down there? Tracks or any sign at all of human activity?"

Choy shook his head. "No. I do most of look. This airplane don't got auto-pilot so Donegan got to watch direction gyro." He nodded his head toward McKeever. "Good mechanic but can't see shit no how."

"Yeah," Fagin said. He tapped the radio. "This doesn't seem to be doing much good."

"Maybe Falconi not turn on radio," Choy said. "Maybe break radio, huh?"

Fagin felt a flash of frustration and anger. "Well, you'd think the dumb bastard would turn on his commo equipment if he heard an airplane."

"Maybe he don't hear us," Choy said. "Maybe we too far away right now. Maybe—"

"Maybe we're flying right over him right now," Fagin said. "Let's get back to work."

"Okay. But we got to turn back in fifteen minutes for Hai-Cat," Choy said. "Airplane run on gasoline, not on air."

"Yeah," Fagin said sarcastically. "It makes you wonder why they don't call it gasoline-plane, don't it?"

Choy thought a moment. "No, I don't wonder. I know why they call it *air*plane."

Fagin sighed at the other's inability to understand sardonic American humor. "We'd better take advantage of these last fifteen minutes," Fagin said.

"You betcha! I already note position for return here tomorrow," Choy said. He started to leave, but turned and placed a hand on Fagin's shoulder. "Don't worry. We keep try to find Falconi."

Although the English was mangled, Fagin appreciated the thought. "By God, Choy, I don't give a damn what Mao Tse-Tung says about you—you're an okay guy!"

Choy was thoughtfully silent for a moment. "Hey! That sumbitch don't know me!"

Now Fagin laughed in spite of his bad mood. "One of these days, I'll sit down and have a long, long talk with you about how Americans joke, Choy."

"I think that's a good idea," Choy said. "You people

all the time say crazy things."

Brigadier General James Taggart, sipping hot coffee in the cool, air-conditioned atmosphere of his office, studied the situation map mounted on the wall.

Filled with blue and red squares drawn on with grease pencil on the acetate overlay, the simple pattern of diagrams that would seem like a rather placid enigma to a casual observer, told a frightening story.

The operations in the Central Highlands weren't going worth a damn.

Unexpected, stiff resistance from North Vietnamese infantry had stopped the effort cold. With the situation muddling up more and more on a daily basis, Viet Cong infiltrators were beginning to move not only between the units committed to the operation there, but had managed to actually penetrate a few of them.

Taggart's G3, a very harried-looking colonel, entered the room with a batch of new SITREPS— Situation Reports. "Good afternoon, sir."

The general said, "How's it going?"

"Well, sir, things haven't exactly all gone to hell but—" The colonel shrugged. "It's close to that now."

"Can we hold our own?"

"Yes, sir. Eventually, but we're going to have to give it everything we've got," the colonel advised him.

"Does that mean committing all our logistics efforts?" Taggart asked.

"We did that two hours ago, sir," the colonel said. "G4 hasn't completed their report on the extent of resupply to units in the field. As soon as I get the official breakdown on numbers and movement I'll let you know."

Taggart nodded. "That mean's I'll have nothing to pull out and give to the guys in Laos."

"You mean the Black Eagles?"

Taggart nodded. "That's exactly who I'm talking about."

The colonel shook his head. "I'm afraid not, sir."

"Damn!" Taggart finished his coffee. "Blanchard!" he hollered.

The outer door opened and a sergeant presented himself with a snappy salute. "Yes, sir?"

"Get word downstairs to that Captain Thuy—you know who I mean."

"The good looking Vietnamese broad that works for Fagin, right, sir?"

"Right. Give her a call and ask her—I say again—*ask* her to come visit me."

Blanchard frowned. "You want me to be nice, sir?"

"Yes, goddamnit, you dumb ass you! I want you to be nice and diplomatic and mannerly or I'll fry your goddamn ass for lunch and ship it down to the Central Highlands."

Blanchard winced visibly. "I'll get her right up here, sir! No sweat!"

The colonel watched the sergeant make a fast exit. "You really want him to be nice?'

"Yeah," Taggart said. "Even I get mellow sometimes when I have to give someone terrible news."

CHAPTER 13

The Pathet Lao infantrymen were bored. Being uneducated men with a great need for external stimulation, the hours on the march had brought them past the point of keeping their mental states awake and interested. Now sunk into thoughtless lethargy, they walked across the Cammon Plateau in front of the T-55 tanks in a condition which Sergeant Major Top Gordon would describe as "having their heads shoved up their asses."

The one exception to this lethargy was their leader, a fiery captain named Namphat. His wakefulness wasn't from a devotion to duty, however. His alertness was due more to the fact he was quite irritated with the Russian tankers and their North Vietnamese Army counterparts.

Namphat had expected to take part in a smashing series of victories that would roll down Laos and into South Vietnam. The huge, noisy, smoking T-55 tanks seemed invincible. But a mysterious group of fighters had not only destroyed several of the big battle wagons but had wiped out a sizeable portion of his own unit. He gave a graphic demonstration of his disenchantment by purposely keeping his men out in front of the armored vehicles. If there were to be any more battles, the Pathet Lao major was determined that he would be responsible for this newly formed alliance's first great victory. He was also less than certain of whether the T-55s would be worth a damn anyway.

While the Pathet Lao captain fumed and stewed, less than a hundred meters away, Lieutenant Colonel Robert Falconi and Sergeant First Class Malpractice McCorkel studied the slowly approaching enemy foot soldiers through their binoculars.

Malpractice licked his dry lips. "They're coming dead on, sir."

"Yeah," Falconi said. "But that's not a usual tank-infantry formation they're using. The riflemen are out in front of the armor instead of using them for cover. I wonder what gives. Maybe they're just a bunch of fuckups."

"It's kind of a good deal for us," Malpractice surmised. "The tankers can't get us without blowing up some of their own men."

"One way or the other, we're going to have a showdown," Falconi said, putting his binoculars away. "And it's gonna be pretty damned quick. I've got to get back to my Charlie Papa. Good luck."

"Same to you, sir," Malpractice said.

Falconi, crawling fast, scurried back to the position where Archie Dobbs was situated. When the Black Eagle commander was in his command post, he quickly checked in with the team leaders over the radio:

"Alpha, Bravo, this is Falcon. We're going to have contact PDQ. Without LAWS we're going to have to

126

rely on the grenadiers as much as we can. The enemy infantry is between us and the tanks. We're going to keep that situation for as long as we can. "Out."

Up on the line, the tired Black Eagles checked the battle sights on their M16s. The two grenadiers— Paulo Garcia and Loco Padilla—loaded M433 anti-personnel and anti-armor grenades into their M203 launchers.

Lieutenant Dimitri Pavlov pulled back on both steering levels bringing the big T-55 to an abrupt halt.

"What's going on?" Krushenko shouted angrily after bumping his head on the bulkhead of the turret. Even with a padded tanker helmet on, it had hurt.

"Ya bolyen," Pavlov said getting out of the driver's seat and pushing his way across the others and up to the hatch. "I am going to vomit."

"Then do it outside!" Brigis said from the gun-loading position. It was bad enough having to stay in the airless tank without having the stench of puke added to the steamy discomfort.

The three sweltering Russians sat in numb misery as they listened to Pavlov gagging outside.

"He is in bad shape," Senior Lieutenant Konstantin Bulovich said to Krushenko. "He is showing every indication of heat stroke."

Krushenko sighed. "You are right, of course. His situation will grow more dangerous if we continue." He took a deep breath. "I am beginning to feel bad myself."

"The only problem is that we are in the middle of

an operation," Bulovich reminded him.

"To *adski* with the operation," Brigis said. "Listen to poor Dimitri throw up."

There was a clanking sound as Pavlov reappeared, dropping weakly back into the interior. *"Prastityi —* I am sorry, comrades," he said in a low voice. "But this awful heat is sapping my strength."

"I think we are going back," Brigis said.

Pavlov, his sallow complexion improved slightly by this sudden good news, looked hopefully at Krushenko. "Is this true?"

"Da," Krushenko said, nodding his head. "But once again we are faced with a damned face-saving situation with those damned Orientals."

Bulovich winked. "I noticed a strange sound in the engines. Perhaps there is dust in the carburetors."

"Yes!" Brigis said. "And weren't those North Vietnamese mechanics charged with tune-ups a few days ago?"

Now Krushenko grinned. "You are right, comrade. I must speak to the senior North Vietnamese officer." He grabbed his microphone and spoke into it, his Russian-accented Vietnamese guttural and harsh. "I must speak to you immediately about a distressing situation, Comrade!" He switched off the set before the NVA officer could reply.

Now displaying a frown of righteous indignation, he raised up in the turret and climbed outside, walking across the apron and dropping to the ground.

The North Vietnamese officer, a young captain, had gotten out of his own vehicle. He approached the Russian, giving a salute. *"Chuyen gi vay?"*

"I'll tell you what is the matter," Krushenko said angrily. "There is sand and dirt in the carburetors!"

The NVA captain shrugged. "Then we will clean them out."

Krushenko shook his head. "We must return to our camp in order to accomplish this. Each carburetor will have to be taken apart, cleaned and oiled, then put back together."

"Let us do this maintenance chore after our operation is brought to a victorious finish," the NVA officer said. There was something about the Russian officer's manner of speech that made him suspicious.

Krushenko shook his head. "If the tanks break down, they will be helpless. The enemy will shoot them up like floating geese on a lake."

"I think the engines sound fine," the North Vietnamese said doggedly.

"Fool! What do you know of such technical things?" Krushenko angrily demanded. He began to feel the NVA officer didn't believe him. "We are all graduates of the Armored Force Academy."

The Vietnamese Red pointed to the Pathet Lao infantry ahead. "What about the Pathet Lao comrades?"

"We will let them go ahead," Krushenko explained. "They can reconnoiter, then return to camp and tell us what they found. We will plan a future operation based on that information."

The North Vietnamese shook his head. "It seems such a waste of time, Comrade."

"You remember that it was *your* crew of mechanics who tuned up the engines," Krushenko said, putting the blame on the NVA. "Talk to them about delays, not me."

The young captain sighed. "Yes, Comrade. I will turn my tanks around and head back."

"We will follow," Krushenko said.

McKeever, his dungarees reeking with the smell of aviation fuel, walked into the bungalow at Hai-Cat. "Okay. She's fueled up for tomorrow's flight," he announced. "I had a little problem with the port engine."

Tim Donegan watched his mechanic walk through the living room and into the kitchen. When McKeever came back out carrying a Guinness Stout, he looked at him. "Well?"

"Well what?" McKeever asked, sitting down on the sofa between Chuck Fagin and Choy.

Donegan leaned forward. "You said you had a little trouble with the port engine."

"Yeah."

"Would you like to tell me about it?" Donegan asked in an exasperated tone.

"Sure," McKeever said. "The oil pressure was down. I had to replace the pump. It's alright now."

"Good," Donegan said leaning back in his chair. "I don't think I'd care to have an engine seize up while flying over Laos."

McKeever missed the point. "I wouldn't want one to seize up no matter where I was flying." He took a sip of the strong drink. "Anyhow, I put a new pump in the starboard engine, too. They both got the same amount o' running time on 'em, so's I figgered the other would be going out, too."

"You know, Mike, you're really smart and logical when it comes to mechanical things," Fagin said. "How come you're so all-fired dumb at everything else?"

"I ain't dumb," McKeever said in a calm voice. "I just don't give a shit 'bout nothing else." Then he grinned. "I was smart enough to charge them two pumps to your account along with the fuel."

"Hey!" Fagin protested. "That's not fair. The damned things would have been replaced anyhow."

Donegan interjected, "Agency policy, Chuck. You know that. If a piece of equipment goes out during an operation, the charge for replacing it comes out of that mission's budget."

"I didn't come down here with unlimited funds," Fagin said. "Give me a break, okay?"

Choy, who was in charge of logistics and funding for the team, had been scribbling in his notebook. "You got enough dough for one trip more, Chuck Fagin. You betcha!"

Fagin's eyes flashed anger. "Then you map out a damned good search for tomorrow, goddamn you!"

Choy nodded. "I want to find them, too, Fagin. Okay? Don't be pissed off on me, huh?"

"We'll do our best, Chuck," Donegan assured him.

McKeever laughed. "I can remember they was times when our best wasn't good enough."

Fagin sneered. "You're a real cheerful bastard, ain't you?"

"Sure," McKeever agreed. "I just got two brand new oil pumps."

Andrea Thuy sat at her desk for a long time. She'd made some sincere attempts to do some work on the documents piled high in her in-box, but she couldn't concentrate on the task.

Brigadier General James Taggart had called her into his office. Unusually civil, the gruff general had invited her to sit down while he gave her some of the worst news she'd ever received in her life.

"Captain Thuy," Taggart had told her. "The operation out in the Central Highlands isn't exactly zipping along according to schedule."

Andrea, sipping the iced tea he had given her, felt a cold stab of apprehension. But she kept her voice under control. "That's bad news, General Taggart. What seems to be the problem?"

"Well," he said from behind his desk. "I guess you're aware that the war isn't real popular with the folks back home."

"Anybody who reads a newspaper knows that," Andrea said, wondering what he was leading up to.

Taggart stood up and walked over to his wet bar. "The bottom line on the situation is that we've got to keep casualties down to a bare minimum."

"It's hard to fight a war without somebody getting killed or wounded, isn't it?"

"It's impossible," Taggart said. He mixed himself a scotch and soda. "But we can keep losses at a minimum if we proceed correctly." He returned to his desk. "Which is exactly what we're doing. Naturally, this policy means the missions take a hell of a lot longer to accomplish while we sort of ease our way to the objectives."

"Yes, General. Please go on," Andrea said.

"If there is any serious resistance at all, we pull back our infantry and send in helicopter gunships and the air force to pound the hell out of enemy positions with everything from napalm, AGM-114 hellfire rockets, FFARs and miniguns," Taggart said. "Naturally it takes time. That means more rations, more weaponry, more ammo, more—," he smiled, "—more of everything actually."

Andrea's patience wore thin. "Look, General. You've already told Fagin and me that Lieutenant

132

Colonel Falconi and the Black Eagles are way, way down on the priority list for munitions and weaponry."

"I did," Taggart agreed.

"I'm not exactly sure what happened, but I understand that some extra funding found itself into Fagin's hands. He is using that until the logistical situation for the Detachment can get back to normal."

"And I'm sure he's using those monies well," Taggart said.

"So what else do you have to tell me?" Andrea said.

Taggart looked straight into her eyes. "The logistical support for the Black Eagles has dried up—permanently."

Andrea jumped to her feet. "You mean they've been abandoned?"

Taggart sighed. "Captain Thuy, when Fagin's funds are used up, there won't be any more."

"Then get Falconi and his men the hell out of there!" Andrea shouted.

"My dear," Taggart said softly. "We can't even do that."

CHAPTER 14

The orders given to Captain Namphat of the Pathet Lao infantry by the Russian officers before they left with the tanks had been explicit:

"Continue the mission as a reconnaissance operation," Krushenko said, emphasizing the importance of what he was saying by shaking his finger in Namphat's face. "When contact with the enemy is made, make a careful note of the location and return immediately to the base camp so the tanks can go out and destroy them."

The Pathet Lao commander, with his trust and confidence in the Russians on the wane, had almost openly sneered. But he retained a passive expression as the instructions were related to him through the interpreter. In the end, he nodded politely and saluted.

Actually, Namphat had every intention of obeying those orders—with the exception of the last part. He was all for seeking out and locating the American outfit that had given his own unit such a terrible mauling. But he sure as hell was not going to pull back and go running to the base camp if he found that enemy group.

The Pathet Lao commander had every intention of crushing them, then returning to report a victory that he was able to achieve without having those noisy, cursed tanks around.

Now, after the delay of having to confer with the talkative, sickly Russians, Namphat and his men once again moved south toward the shadows of the distant mountain.

While the Pathet Lao infantry renewed their slow march, Archie Dobbs watched their movement carefully. Falconi had ordered him forward to establish an observation post. But rather than having a protective position, all Archie could do was keep himself as flat to the ground as possible.

At first he used his binoculars, but when they drew close enough he could recognize their facial features, the Black Eagle scout knew the field glasses were no longer needed.

"Falcon," he said into his radio, "this is Scout. They're closing in and headed straight this way as sure as shit stinks. But at least them tanks is gone. Over."

"Say again," Falconi replied. "The tanks are gone?"

"Affirmative," Archie answered. "At least I can't see the bastards right now."

Falconi lying in his primitive command post answered, "Roger, Scout. Keep me informed. Out." The detachment commander gave the situation a quick going-over in his mind.

His men, although camouflaged and relatively safe from observation at a distance, were in a position that would be difficult to defend. He didn't know what mysterious reason caused the tanks to pull out, but while that made the situation less difficult, it didn't guarantee an easy battle. The approaching enemy was well armed and more numerous than his men. Once the bad guys reached a point short of fifty meters of his position, they would spot the Black Eagles. No doubt, they would launch an immediate assault forcing the Detachment into a difficult defensive posture.

In Lieutenant Colonel Robert Falconi's mind, there was only one thing to do:

"Alpha, Bravo," he said into his radio, "this is Falcon. Prepare to attack. On my command have each grenadier fire two M397 airburst grenades. Scout, pull back. Out."

Archie Dobbs, in his forward position, didn't bother to acknowledge the transmission. He knew damned well that time was not to be wasted in a situation like the present one. He scurried back deeper into the depression, then turned and headed for Falconi as fast as he could crawl.

While Archie was getting back to his position, Paulo Garcia and Loco Padilla, each with their respective assault teams, slipped airburst projectiles into their grenade launchers. The two marines also placed another one nearby to instantly fire after the first was shot.

When Archie joined his commander, he turned around and once again faced the enemy. "There's more'n a hunnerd out there, sir."

"All Pathet Lao?" Falconi asked.

"Yes, sir. I didn't see any NVA or Viet Cong," Archie replied. "I kinda wished there was some with 'em. They keep them Laotian Reds simmered down some."

Falconi displayed a grim smile. "Yeah. We've fought those bastards before, haven't we?"

"Yes, sir. And not too far from here if I remember

right."

"You remember correctly," Falconi said. "It was on the mission when we infiltrated in a glider."

"Right, sir. The one where we knocked out the Red nuclear power plant."

Now Falconi could see the first rank of enemy riflemen appearing on the horizon where the basin's rim was located. He pressed the transmit button. "Alpha, Bravo, alert the grenadiers. Wait."

The gravity of the situation was not lost on Archie. "This is going to be real hairy."

Falconi acknowledged the remark with a nod of his head. He let a few seconds slip by. "Prepare to fire." Less than a half minute later, at least fifty of the advancing Pathet Lao could be seen. Falconi took a deep breath. "Fire!"

Two simultaneous "whumps" from the M203s sounded to the front. The grenades launched upward in the trajectories that resulted from the skillful aim of the two marine sergeants.

The enemy in the front rank stumbled to a ragged halt at the sound of the launchers' going off. An instant later, the grenades hit the ground then bounced back up five feet before detonating.

The two explosions sliced into the Pathet Lao, bowling over the men at the head of their ragged column. Those unlucky troops rolled to the ground in bloody heaps. Captain Namphat reacted quickly, eagerly, and correctly.

"Attack!" he shrieked loudly. Like his men, he was a zealot. As the firing increased, so did his excitement. He advanced so rapidly that he began to pass up his own soldiers. "Attack! Attack!"

Ray Swift Elk's Alpha Assault Team held the left of the Black Eagle line. He had situated his men so that they curved around slightly forming a small pocket. The extreme outside of this flank was held by Blue Richards and Calvin Culpepper. Calvin, on full-automatic, hosed sprays of 5.56-millimeter slugs at the enemy while Blue punctuated those rapid fire bursts with skillfully aimed and spaced single shots.

Meanwhile the rest of the team—Swift Elk, Paulo, and Steve Matsuno—cut loose with their own fusillades that resulted in catching the attackers in a shallow, but effective crossfire.

A dozen Pathet Lao toppled to the ground under the storm of bullets that ploughed into their tight attack formation. But others, not bothered by the thoughts of their potential deaths, pressed on to continue the hysterical assault.

Top Gordon's Bravos were not exactly sitting around with their thumbs up their asses either. Top, a veteran of more conventional airborne units, believed in plenty of fire and artillery support. Without mortars or howitzers to back him up, the sergeant major used Loco Padilla's M230 to the best advantage.

Unlike Paulo, Loco didn't use his M16. He fired methodically into the attackers, hitting first one side of their line, the other side, and finally the center as he sent numerous small burst of anti-personnel shrapnel slashing through the Pathet Lao.

While this one-man mini-artillery blasted away, the others in the detachment backed up Malpractice McCorkel. Like Calvin in the Alphas, Malpractice did his deadly work with his selector pushed to full-auto. Quick, lethal salvos from his rifle crumbled numerous attackers while the other Bravos fired fast semi-auto volleys into the bellowing horde of Red fanatics.

Yet Captain Namphat's unit pressed on down into the basin, hoping to overwhelm the Black Eagles by numbers alone. The sight of their own dead seemed to inflame their battle ardor.

Falconi had a good view of the battle. Between that advantage and his profound combat leadership experience, he could tell that the Detachment could hold off the attackers for another ten minutes maximum.

It was time to change tactics.

"Alpha," he radioed. "Start pulling rearward. Do it slow and deliberate. "Bravo, cover 'em. Go! Go! Go!"

Ray Swift Elk immediately went into action. "Steve! Blue! Move back!"

Without asking why, the two Black Eagles got up into crouching positions and moved backward. They still fired into the enemy as they traveled backward.

"Okay, Calvin and Paulo. Shit and git!" Swift Elk yelled.

The senior rifleman and grenadier now imitated the other two. They withdrew, yet kept a curtain of flying slugs out to their direct front.

When his team was realigned, Swift Elk brought them to a halt. Once again they formed a formidable line against the Pathet Lao.

Now Top began a retrograde movement.

Doing exactly as Swift Elk had done, a pair of his men started the withdrawal, then were joined by the others. The Bravos went back farther than the Alphas so that they could cover them for the next pullback.

When the Alphas renewed the rearward maneuver, Falconi and Archie went to the front line to aid in covering fire. Their M16s blasted together, adding an enfilading fire to the overall efforts of the Detachment.

Now the Pathet Lao's attack began to stumble a bit. A few minutes before, they'd been able to sweep forward over their own dead. But this new tactic gave much more concentrated incoming fire. Instead of pushing ahead, they were slowed by the sudden influx of cadavers that were stacking up in the middle of their tactical efforts. The more they slowed down, the more of them died.

Finally, Captain Namphat came to his senses.

"Section leaders! Align your men!" he screamed. He now realized that his assault formation was no more than a milling mob, hopelessly caught in highly skilled defensive salvos that were tearing the hell out of them. When he still sustained heavy casualties even after reforming his unit, the Pathet Lao officer did something very unusual for the style of fighting his army generally participated in.

"Stand fast! Halt the attack!"

A few of the more fanatical men refused to obey. They continued going forward, climbing and stumbling over the pile of dead in front of them. When they reached the forward portion of the cadavers, the massed fire of the defenders slammed into them with a deadly force and they collapsed into the bloody pile of dead humanity.

Namphat shrieked at his section leaders to gain control over their men. This was made difficult by the fact that, like their commanding officer, these NCOs had also gone crazy during the attack. There was no unit integrity among the survivors, but Namphat threatened and screamed until a semblance of order finally came out of the chaos.

The Pathet Lao drew back to regroup. Because of the terrain and the stack of bodies, the Black Eagles

140

lost sight of their attackers. Falconi was plainly worried. "I've never known them to break off an assault before."

"Me either," Archie agreed.

Falconi raised his head to take a look at the two teams. Both were in tact. The leaders, Swift Elk and Top, waved at him to let the CO know that they were still in good shape.

The lieutenant colonel gestured back at them. "They're probably as curious as we are about how the situation is shaping up. The Pathet Lao might have called the fight off, but I doubt it."

Archie winked at Falconi. "Sir, this looks like a job for Super Scout."

"Go for it, Hero," Falconi said.

"Just call me Captain Recon." Archie raised himself into a crouch, then hurried forward to the edge of the basin. When he reached the high ground, he threw himself down and crawled up to the dead enemy. He found a spot where he was able to peer between a couple of sprawled individuals who had caught more than their share of Black Eagle bullets.

"Oh, shit!"

Archie backed away, then stood up and ran as fast as he could. "Here they come!" He continued until he flung himself down beside Falconi.

"Archie, what—"

All other conversation was cut off by the abrupt appearance of Pathet Lao infantrymen leaping over the piles of bodies. They hit the edge of the depression and raced down toward the Black Eagles.

Trigger fingers pumped, grenades were launched, and streams of bullets roared out of the defenders' position. The Red riflemen stormed into the metal hell, going down in screaming shrieks like stalks of

141

wheat falling in front of an invisible combine.

"Kill the bastards or die yourselves!" Top bellowed. "Goddamn it, Loco! More airbursts out front!"

The deafening noise of the battle built up to a continuous detonation of blasting M16s and AK47s. The Pathet Lao died by the dozen, tumbling and stumbling to the ground in bursts and salvos of bullets streaming into their midst. Their storming assault quickly thinned out until the last six men went down together, cut to ribbons by a combination of small arms and grenade shrapnel.

Suddenly — silence.

The smell of cordite hung heavy in the air and the men could barely hear because of their punished eardrums. Lieutenant Colonel Robert Falconi's voice seemed muted and hollow as he gave his vocal orders:

"Those tanks will be back anytime. Team leaders take charge of your men and move 'em out. We've got to get the hell out of here."

"Where in blazes are we going, sir?" Archie asked wanting to know what direction to go.

"The tanks went that way," Falconi answered pointing. "So we'll go this way."

"They'll catch up, sir," Archie said. "Then what'll we do?"

Falconi shrugged. "You never figured on living forever anyway, did you?"

CHAPTER 15

Pink rays of the setting sun shot through the navigator's observation window on the port side of the PBY. It gave the interior of the aircraft a rosy glow.

Chuck Fagin grimaced at this undeniable sign of the end of the day. He grasped the microphone, speaking with a tone of desperation in his voice:

"Falcon, this is Aircraft. Over. Falcon, this is Aircraft. Over."

Mike McKeever, doing as he usually did when he hadn't anything important or particular to do, snoozed against the opposite bulkhead. His head rolled gently with the movements of the aircraft as it cruised through the heavy atmosphere of the tropical sky. Fagin, with empty air hissing in his earphones, found the sight of the sleeping mechanic irritating as hell.

The hatchway leading to the cockpit opened and Choy made an appearance. The expression on his usually inscrutable face was one of regret and sadness. "Hello, Fagin."

"Get outta here, Choy!" Fagin snapped. Knowing that the navigator came with bad news, he pushed the transmit button again. "Falcon, this is Aircraft. Over."

"Fagin, Donovan say we go back now."

"Bullshit!"

"No bullshit, Fagin," Choy said. He held up his slide rule. "I work up all calculations on distance and gasoline. We turn back in five minutes or we crash in jungle before we reach Hai-Cat."

"Piss on your slide rule!" Fagin snarled.

The Chinese navigator quickly shoved the instrument into the side pocket of his flight suit. "Hey! Don't piss on my slide rule. You crazy?"

"Maybe you made a mistake," Fagin suggested hopefully. "Check your figures again, okay?"

"I am professional," Choy said. "In school I win all the prizes in mathematics." He shrugged. "Sorry. Sorry. It all simple. No chance for mistake."

Fagin sighed. "Shit!"

"We got to go back. I sorry, Fagin. Really sorry. Okay?"

Fagin calmed down. He nodded his head. "Okay. I guess there wouldn't be a hell of a lot to gain by running out of fuel and smashing into the trees, huh?"

"I can't think of nothing," Choy said seriously.

Chuck Fagin knew that the operation to find Falconi and the Black Eagles was over. He was out of funds, out of time, and out of luck. If Falconi knew enough about the real situation and that he wasn't going to be resupplied, he could escape and evade his way back to friendly territory. He might lose half his men between the Cammon Plateau and the Central Highlands, but at least some of them would make it. Unfortunately, however, the Black Eagle commander was operating under the assumption that some sort of logistical and weapon support was headed his way. He would conduct his tactics and the mission's operations on the condition he was to be resupplied.

The big airplane went into a gentle bank, turning south before straightening out. Choy nodded his head. "That all, Fagin. We go back now. Sorry. Sorry."

"It's a sorry goddamned world," Fagin said under his breath. He angrily slammed the microphone back into its holder on the radio. Then he pulled the earphones off and tossed them across the fuselage so hard that it woke up McKeever.

The large man yawned. "What's going on?"

"Shut your fucking mouth or I'll kick your ass but good," Fagin yelled. He didn't give a damn about McKeever's size or the fact the man could whip him like a stepchild. Fagin was aching for a fight.

McKeever sensed the tenseness in the air. "I ain't looking for no trouble." He wasn't particularly upset about the prospect of getting into a fight. In fact, he always enjoyed a good donnybrook. McKeever just wasn't in the mood to work up a sweat at that particular time.

Choy shook his head. "Calm down, everybody. I go back to cockpit." The Chinese navigator patted Fagin on the shoulder, then returned to join Tim Donegan.

McKeever knew that Fagin was upset about not being able to locate Falconi and the Black Eagles. However, with his range of emotions as limited as his intellect, the mechanic didn't really appreciate the emotional pain of the other man. But he did sense Fagin needed cheering up, so he brought up the one subject he always found spiritually uplifting.

"Hey, Fagin," McKeever said. "Think about the Guinness Stout waiting for us back at Hai-Cat."

Fagin smiled weakly. "Yeah."

"We got plenty," McKeever reminded him.

"Okay." Now that he'd calmed down, Fagin was glad McKeever hadn't decided to punch it out with him.

Up in the cockpit, Donegan carefully followed Choy's plotted course. Gently working wheel and rudder pedals, he turned east and south. After an hour, the South China Sea was a blue haze on the horizon. "Too bad about Fagin," Donegan said.

Choy sighed. "Too bad about Falconi. Always too bad when a good man die, huh?"

"Yeah," Donegan said. "There's been a hell of a lot of that out here in Southeast Asia lately — good men dying."

"That the way of war," Choy said.

"I wish there was some way we could get some gasoline for some more trips."

"No can do," Choy said. "All chits used up."

The two remained sullen and silent for the remainder of the trip. By the time Donegan pushed the control column forward for the final descent, darkness was rapidly overcoming that part of the world. Gradually losing altitude, a few minutes passed before the PBY gently slapped against the waves, then settled down for the spray-throwing taxi up to the dock. McKeever crawled out onto the bow of the plane, grabbing the mooring line and leaping onto pier to tie them up.

Donegan cut the engines. He sat still for several long moments. "I feel lousy."

"Me too," Choy said. He pointed at McKeever standing on the dock. "He is happy."

146

"Happy and dumb," Donegan said.

"That the way to be," Choy said. "No have to think, huh?"

"Yeah," Donegan said. "C'mon. Let's get over to the bungalow and wrap up this shitty day."

"I try to think of some Oriental philosophy for this situation," Choy said. "But nothing come to mind. Centuries of wisdom wasted — like Black Eagle lives."

Fagin joined them. "That's that."

"Yeah," Donegan agreed. "That is most definitely that."

Five minutes later the four men strolled slowly up the pathway leading to the aircrew's quarters. As they approached the building they could see the figure of a man sitting on the sofa inside.

"We got a visitor," Donegan said.

"I hope he don't want no Guinness," McKeever said without charity.

They went inside the billets and stopped at the sight of someone they hadn't seen in a long, long time.

Clayton Andrews, senior CIA officer and the original founder of the Black Eagles, stood up to greet them. "It looks like you boys got back in just the nick of time," Andrews said. "Five more minutes and this place would've been too dark for a safe landing."

"We woulda set down at sea and waited for morning," Donegan said. "That's the advantage of an amphibious aircraft."

Fagin walked up to his old friend and offered his hand. "It's been awhile, Andy. Remember Choy and McKeever?"

"Sure," Andrews answered. "How're you boys doing?" He took Fagin by the arm and led him toward the door. "I want to talk to you." He looked back at the others. "Excuse me, guys, okay?"

"Sure," Donegan said.

They went outside and Andrews said, "I heard you've been running flights looking for Falconi."

"Yeah, Andy," Fagin said. "He and the Detachment got suddenly cut off when an operation in the Central Highlands was given top priority."

"I know," Andy said. "I got the word on it a couple of days ago. Naturally I was interested in what was going down in the mission, so I looked into it."

"Understandable," Fagin remarked.

"I looked *deep* into it," Andy added.

Fagin nervously licked his lips. "Uh, yeah."

"From what I found out, I would have written the operation, Falconi, the Black Eagles, and everything off," Andy said, beginning to pace back and forth. "But then I heard you were running flights in an attempt to locate them."

"Sure. I couldn't hang 'em out to dry, could I?"

"I even heard you had supplies ready to drop to them. Is that right?" Andy inquired.

"Of course. Finding Falconi would have been useless if I couldn't help him out."

"Chuck, we didn't have any funding for resupply," Andy said.

"Sure we did."

"Bullshit!"

"Have you heard of any stolen money or even any *mis*appropriated funds?" Fagin asked.

"No," Andy admitted. "But I've seen your budget and you had used it all up, Chuck. There wasn't an extra dime in your operational account to pedal a bicycle across the street. Yet you've managed a couple of resupply flights and even the material to parachute in." Andrews paused a moment, looking straight into his subordinate's face. "Out with it. How'd you do it?"

"Magic," Fagin said. He grinned and shrugged. "I swear to you, Andy. It wasn't stolen." He shrugged. "What the hell difference does it make now? It's used up and Falconi is still out there somewhere."

"You're not BSing me about the dough not being swiped, are you?" Andrews asked.

Fagin raised his hand. "It was not—I swear!"

"You've got something against stolen money, Chuck?"

Fagin feigned surprise. "Of course! I'm not called Honest Chuck Fagin for nothing."

Andy shook his head. "Tsk! Tsk! That's too bad. Because I've got fifty thousand dollars that I swiped."

Fagin's mouth dropped open. He stared at the other CIA man then burst out laughing. "You're beautiful! You're goddamned beautiful!" He lowered his voice. "Where'd you get it?"

"Ask me no questions and I'll tell you no lies," Andy said. He looked around. "This Hai-Cat is a nice place."

Fagin nodded. "Yeah. It used to be a French Army R&R center for officers."

"You like it?"

"Sure," Fagin answered. "Let's get back to the subject of the money you have."

"One thing at a time," Andy said. "By the way, I'm happy to hear you like it at Hai-Cat, because you're stationed here now," Andy said. "Andrea is on her way down with your office supplies—desks, file cabinets, and all." Andy winked. "I thought it best that we avoid Peterson Field for awhile."

"Peterson Field? Or Brigadier General James Taggart?" Fagin asked.

"Like I said, pal, ask me no questions and I'll tell you no lies," Andrews said.

"Let's get back and let Donegan and his crew know what's happening," Fagin said.

"Yeah," Andy said. "And I've got a special briefing to give them."

The two returned to the bungalow. The flight crew, sensing something was up, gave the two CIA officers silent, close gazes. Clayton Andrews didn't waste any time. "The operation to find Falconi isn't over," he announced.

Donegan took a long pull on his Guinness. "I assume you got some more dough to throw into the project, right?"

"Right."

McKeever, dull-eyed and unimpressed, said, "I'll need a chit for gasoline tomorrow."

"You'll have it," Andrews promised.

"So what's the word on tomorrow's flight?" Donegan asked.

"Yeah," Choy said. "Tell me destination so I can plot course. Okay, Andy?"

"Okay," Andrews said. "The agenda is simple. We'll just continue the search pattern you guys were following. Does that sound logical?"

"Yeah," Fagin said. "But we weren't following any set schedule or checking out particular places on the fly-overs. We had limited time, so we made some wide runs hoping the radio would make up any problems in distance." He shrugged. "Unfortunately, Falconi only has Prick-Sixes. Even if he heard us—and I doubt he did—there was always the chance he couldn't reach us with those little commo sets."

"Okay then," Andrews said. "We'll tighten things down, but make some sweeps over parts of the

Cammon Plateau you haven't covered yet. If we can't raise him, then we'll work our way back to the opposite side of the place."

The realization of the situation finally hit Fagin. He burst out laughing. "Goddamn it! I suddenly feel pretty good. Where's that Guinness Stout?"

"Take it easy," McKeever said. "There ain't much."

Fagin frowned at him. "In the plane you said there was plenty."

"In the plane I din't know you was so thirsty," McKeever said.

"Bullshit!" Donegan said. "We've got cases of it out there. Drink all you want, Fagin."

Fagin grinned. "I goddamned well intend to!"

CHAPTER 16

Sergeant Major Top Gordon bit the tip off a fresh cigar. He spat it out. "I'd like to know what the hell is going on." He lit the stogie and exhaled a cloud of pungent smoke, wiping at the rivulets of sweat that coursed down his rugged face. "Something ain't kosher, that's for sure."

The Black Eagles' senior non-commissioned officer was sitting within a small grove of thick green jungle fern with Lieutenant Colonel Robert Falconi and First Lieutenant Ray Swift Elk. Archie Dobbs relaxed a few meters away, lazily listening to the conference going on between the commander and the two assault team leaders. The remainder of the Detachment was spread out in strategic defensive locations along the edge of the mangrove swamp where Falconi had moved them after the battle with the Pathet Lao.

"There should have been a resupply drop," Swift Elk said. "The time frame wasn't tight, but we were at the drop zone long enough to make up for any delays in getting a flight out to us."

"Ammo is going to be a problem pretty damned quick," Top said.

"Well," Swift Elk said. "We've stolen from the enemy before. AK47s are as familiar to us as these babies." He patted his M16.

"Rations will be the next consideration," Top said.

"Hell," Falconi scoffed. "We're sitting in the middle of a salad right now." He grabbed one of the fern leaves and pulled it free. Biting into it, he said, "It's nutritious and tastes a little like asparagus."

"I know that, sir," Top said. "And the fronds are good for constructing shelters and hootches. But I ain't a vegetarian. If noise security won't let me shoot game, I'll settle for meat out of a can. When there ain't any of that, I get in a bad mood."

"If we had some decent goddamned radios we could talk to somebody," Swift Elk said. "As it is, we can't make contact unless we're within range of the Prick-Sixes."

"I'm thinking this is going to be the last goddamned time we come out here without a good commo set," Falconi said.

"What the hell's the difference, sir?" Top said. "We ain't even seen any aircraft around anyhow."

"I don't know what we're making such a big deal about. This situation isn't that new to us," Falconi said. "Either there's been a big foul-up or we've been hung out to dry."

"The big problem is having to deal with Russian armor," Swift Elk said. "We could manage if there was nothing but Pathet Lao or NVA infantry around. But eventually, those tanks are going to catch us good. The odds are against us."

"I'm not convinced our predicament is impossible yet. Maybe the brass can get their act together before long," Falconi said. "So I'm willing to give this mission another twenty-four hours before I start thinking in a negative fashion."

"Yes, sir," Swift Elk said. "But that doesn't make conducting this mission any easier."

Top shoved the cigar between his teeth. "Especially when we take into account that we're on foot in a mechanized war."

Swift Elk grinned. "We're like the one-legged man in a kicking contest, aren't we?"

Falconi chuckled. "Or the guy that showed up at the ax fight without an ax."

"You two are real funny," Top said.

Archie Dobbs called over softly. "I got an idea."

All three turned toward the scout. Top scowled. "This I gotta hear."

"I think we oughta steal one o' them Russian tanks," Archie said.

"Are you outta your mind?" Top snarled.

"No. I could hotwire it," Archie responded. "Hell, I been doing that since the sixth grade."

"That's real admirable," Top said. "But you don't have to hot wire tanks. They got ignition switches. You don't even need a goddamned key."

Falconi was thoughtful for a few minutes. "Sometimes Archie is so crazy he's smart."

"Whattaya mean, sir?" Top asked incredulously. "Are you saying you think this crazy bastard has come up with a good idea?"

"Maybe," Falconi mused. "Let me do a little thinking out loud here. Suppose we organize a combat patrol?" He laughed. "Or maybe I should say a tank-stealing patrol? Archie would go, naturally—"

"Naturally!" Archie exclaimed.

"Blue Richards would be a good man," Falconi said. "After spending most of his boyhood transporting white lightning on Georgia back roads, he can drive anything.

"Yes, sir," Swift Elk agreed. "He did a damned good job on that APC during the last operation."

"Paulo Garcia and his M203 might come in handy in the event things went to hell," Falconi continued.

"And they will, sir. Count on it," Top interjected.

Archie had a suggestion. "We'd need a good gunner for the tank's weaponry, sir. Gunnar Olson is our man for that."

"Yeah," Falconi said in agreement. He motioned to Archie. "Get Blue, Gunnar, and Paulo. Tell them to report over here in patrol harness only."

"Yes, sir!" Archie exclaimed getting to his feet. "Now this goddamned mission is going somewhere!"

Andrea Thuy looked around the spacious bungalow. "So this is home now, huh?"

She and Chuck Fagin stood in the outer office of their new headquarters at Hai-Cat. Chuck smiled. "It's a hell of a lot nicer than Peterson Field, ain't it?"

"I'm going to miss my apartment in Saigon," Andrea said. "I'd really grown into it."

"Jesus!" Fagin scoffed. "You're out in the country here. The beach is a stone's throw away, it's quieter, cooler, and definitely safer than Saigon."

"That apartment was the first real home I've ever known, Chuck," Andrea said.

"It was cramped and in a crowded neighborhood," Fagin pointed out. "You can make that little house they've given you here into a much nicer place."

"I know," Andrea said. "But it won't be the same."

"And isn't the UNESCO orphanage where your friend Uzuri works nearby?" Fagin asked.

"Yes. It's only a couple of kilometers down the

road," Andrea said. "It's nice to be close to her, I'll admit that."

"You haven't had very many women friends, have you?"

"Just Betty Lou Pemberton and Malpractice's wife Jean," Andrea said. "Betty Lou went back to the States, but Jean is coming out to work at the orphanage now that the detachment is going to be stationed here."

"That's great!" Fagin exclaimed. "When Jean gets here, you'll have two female buddies available for hen parties."

Jean McCorkel, the Vietnamese wife of the Black Eagle medic, was a fully qualified nurse. She'd met Malpractice during the mission on the Song Cai River. Top Gordon was badly wounded and the two operated on the sergeant major, saving his life. They continued working together and eventually fell in love. They were married immediately after the campaign on the river was brought to a successful conclusion.

Fagin glanced around the office. "The furniture is all in place now. Is there anything else I can do for you?"

Andrea shook her head. "I can do the finishing up. Have the supplies from Clayton Andrews arrived?"

"Yeah," Fagin answered. "Donegan called me earlier this afternoon. They just came in. I'm going down to the dock now to help him and his two partners-in-crime load up the aircraft."

Andrea noted the lateness of the day. "It will be dark soon."

"There're lights down there," Fagin said. "We'll finish up tonight, then take off at first light. We should be over the Cammon Plateau by 0700."

"God!" Andrea said with a sigh. "I hope you find the Black Eagles soon."

"Don't worry," he said. He walked to the door. "Don't get down in the dumps, huh? It don't do no good."

"Don't worry about me," Andrea said.

"Right, kid. I'll see you later."

"I'll stay here until you've finished," Andrea said. "Come on back for a nightcap."

"Sure," Fagin agreed. "We'll drink to success for tomorrow's mission."

"Yes," Andrea said. "And to luck for Falconi and the guys."

"It's all the same, my dear," Fagin said leaving the office. "Without luck there's no success and without success there's no luck."

Captain Chin Hoa, the official NVA interpreter assigned to the Russian tank officers, walked up to the thatched hut that served as their office and living quarters. The North Vietnamese officer rapped on the door and stepped inside.

"Dobriy vechir," he said in Russian. "How are the comrades this evening?"

The senior Soviet officer, Captain Anatol Krushenko, looked up from the book he was reading. "We are fine. Have you received any intelligence on the other comrades?"

"The Pathet Lao?" Chin asked. "We have heard nothing."

Pavel Brigis, relaxing on his bunk, sat up and leaned on his elbow. "What about the sound of distant firing? That was a battle, was it not?"

"Yes, Comrade Lieutenant Brigis," Chin said. "There is no doubt of that."

"Then send a section of troops to investigate," Brigis said.

Chin shrugged. "We have no troops to send, Comrade. All the Pathet Lao went with Captain Namphat."

Lieutenant Dimitri Pavlov, who was beginning to recover from his heat stroke, still felt weak. He, like Brigis, was on his bunk. "Comrade Captain Chin," he said. "Why not send a tank to scout the area?"

Chin shrugged. "They were all inoperative, Comrade."

"*All* of them?" Krushenko demanded to know.

"Yes. Remember. You had us tear down the carburetors," Chin said.

"*Proklinat!*" Krushenko cursed. "I did not mean all of them at once! You never disable all your vehicles at one time any more than you have your men disassemble their weapons for cleaning all at once. It leaves you defenseless."

Chin spoke in an indignant tone. "Your orders were to take the carburetors apart. This we did, Comrade Captain."

Krushenko, knowing what the NVA officer said was true, sighed. "Very well."

"I wish to state, Comrade Captain, that we found no dirt in the machinery," Chin said.

Krushenko felt a flush of embarrassed anger. The whole idea of accusing the NVA tankers of poor maintenance had been a ploy to get himself and his fellow Europeans out of the hot weather and the discomfort it caused them. He sputtered then exclaimed, "We know for certain that there was dirt in our particular carburetor!"

"I beg to differ, Comrade," Chin said. "We took your engine down first."

"I say the machinery was contaminated with foreign matter," Krushenko insisted. "The engine ran rough—"

"I tested it personally," Chin said angrily. "Your tank was in perfect tune and hitting on all cylinders."

Krushenko said nothing for a few moments. When he did speak, his voice was cold. "It would appear, Comrade Captain Chin Hoa, that the Soviet Army style of discipline is needed here."

"I speak only the truth," Chin said.

Krushenko got to his feet. "I will not tolerate insolence in any form! Return to the tanks. Reassemble all carburetors, reinstall them, and make sure the vehicles are properly topped off with diesel fuel and motor oil. You are dismissed."

Chin saluted. *"Da, Tovarish Kapitan!"*

Krushenko returned the salute and said nothing as the NVA captain left the hut. Then he turned to his fellow officers. "Do you suppose the little bastard will make a report?"

Senior Lieutenant Konstantin Bulovich shrugged. "And what if he does? All administrative matters must be submitted through us, *nyet?*"

"Durak! Don't you think the North Vietnamese Army has its own system of bureaucracy?" Krushenko said. He looked at Pavlov. "How are you feeling?"

Pavlov sensed the situation was serious. In the Soviet Army, officers are shot at certain times if they are derelict in their duties. He felt a sudden urge of patriotism. "Do not worry, Comrade Captain Krushenko. I will be able to perform my duties. I shall not fail Mother Russia."

Krushenko switched his gaze to Bulovich. "And you?"

Bulovich leaped to his feet and stood at attention. "I am a loyal son of Mother Russia."

Brigis also got off his bunk. "I, as a Latvian, am a steadfast and trustworthy nephew."

Krushenko scowled. *"Korozhi!* We cannot again falter like we did during the last mission. From this point on, we must push ourselves and our tank to the utmost effort until the Americans are wiped out."

"We will not fail, Comrade," Bulovich assured him.

"We have no choice," Krushenko reminded him. "We must keep foremost in our thoughts that it is a question of their survival or ours."

Pavlov's physical recovery, though psychological, was every much as real as if he'd been given a miracle drug to combat sickness from hot weather. "I swear by the Red Banner to kill the Americans!"

"I swear!" Bulovich echoed.

"And I swear!" Brigis assured his Soviet comrades.

Krushenko understood and appreciated the sincerity of the vow. "The Americans," he said, "are as good as dead this very minute!"

CHAPTER 17

The black clouds floated slowly and eerily across the night sky. Although these patches of aerial vapor were scattered, they were heavy with tropical moisture. The moon, large and pale, had been obscured for almost three quarters of an hour when the cloud bank covering it finally eased farther on its celestial journey toward the Luang Prabang Mountains. This exposed the moon and its light suddenly flooded the Cammon Plateau.

Archie Dobbs froze as he was abruptly bathed in the yellow glare.

Directly behind him, Falconi also stopped moving. He and the others slowly lowered themselves to the ground. The whole patrol was illuminated and exposed to even casual view.

Paulo Garcia, as the tail man in the patrol, glanced backward to make sure there was no one to spot them from that direction. A few moments passed before the Black Eagles were certain they had not been seen in the sudden exposure of moonlight.

The five men from the Detachment had spent a grueling, slow, carefully paced journey traveling

161

from the mangrove swamp toward their destination — which was completely unknown to them. The only sure intelligence they had acquired about the location of the enemy had been the knowledge of the direction from which attacks had been launched at them.

Archie Dobbs, like a cat always able to land on its feet, moved with his unerring instinct toward the northeast. They would know when they reached their objective when an enemy garrison with tanks came into view.

And the Black Eagles' lives depended on being able to see the bad guys first.

Archie felt confident to renew their journey even though the light was still bright. He looked back and signaled to the others, then renewed the trek at a crouch. It was an uncomfortable way to travel, but they had no choice. Twenty minutes later, however, relief came in the form of another opaque cloud bank which drifted across the moon, once again bringing blessed darkness to the area.

Another hour of the slow but steady journey took them across a wide, open expanse and down into a creek bed. Archie noted that the waterway ran in the direction he wanted to go. He took advantage of the cover it offered by leading the patrol through the cycads trees along the bank. The next time the moon shown, it did not affect the security of the patrol.

By the time they reached the point where the creek turned off to the southeast, it was once again dark enough to be able to move out onto the flatlands without fear of discovery. But great care was still exercised. Several times in the following hour,

Archie signaled a halt, then moved forward to personally check out the ground they would be covering. One man scouting around made a hell of a lot less noise than having five pairs of jungle boots treading across the hardpacked soil.

Each of Archie's personnel reconnoiters showed empty countryside, and the patrol continued its movement toward the unknown destination.

Finally, an hour after leaving the creek, the tank engines were heard over the horizon.

Archie Dobbs held up their progress once again and went back to confer with Falconi. The scout pointed directly north. "That's where they are, sir. I'd estimate they're five kilometers away."

"Yeah," Falconi agreed. "Do you think they're coming this way?"

Archie shook his head. "No, sir. In fact, they ain't going no place. Them engines is just being gunned."

Falconi listened for a few moments. "Yeah. Sounds like they're being worked on. It would appear that preventive maintenance is on their schedule." He looked at his watch. "Though it seems late as hell to be doing that sort of work."

Archie grinned. "You reckon they're tuning 'em up for us?"

"One way or the other," Falconi said. "If they're doing any tune-ups or overhauls it's for an operation. And I'd say it's a mission they're going on."

"In that case, they might be leaving at dawn," Archie said.

Blue, Gunnar and Paulo joined them. Paulo reported in. "The rear is secure, sir."

Gunnar listened to the tank engines. The sound was now a familiar one to every Black Eagle. "It don't seem like they're going anywhere."

"We think they're working on 'em," Archie said. "Prob'ly pulling the North Vietnamese version of motor PM on 'em."

"Listen up, guys," Falconi said. "If they're planning on moving out, they'll wait for dawn. I don't think they're crazy enough to drive around here when it's dark."

"But we are, ain't we, sir?" Blue Richards said.

"Yeah," Falconi said. "Anyway, we don't have much choice. We're going to have to get in there, silently knock off any security we run into—I say again—*silently* knock off any security we run into, get a tank, and haul ass in it."

Archie reached down into his boot scabbard and pulled out his stiletto. The knife's blade was as sharp as possible, able to cut paper by simply being gently laid across the edge of a sheet. "I'm ready, sir."

"Okay, Archie. As usual, you'll lead us in. If they keep gunning those engines, it'll make things easier."

"Yes, sir," Paulo Garcia said. "But remember, if they're pulling PM on them tanks, they'll have the place lit up like a Christmas tree."

Blue Richards, thinking of his driving assignment once one of the armored battle wagons was in their possession, said, "Okay. When we pick one, I go in first. You guys move right smartly, on account of I ain't waiting for nothing. I'll punch up the engine if it ain't running, then hit the accelerator and haul balls."

"Do you remember what Top said about steering?" Falconi asked.

"Yes, sir. No wheel, just a coupla levers like on a

bulldozer. No sweat, sir. I've driven some of them, too."

Falconi laughed. "Is there any vehicle you haven't driven, Blue?"

"A Greyhound bus, sir," Blue quickly answered. "And I've always had a crazy yen to drive one."

"You'd think a Soviet T55 tank would make up for that, wouldn't you?" Falconi said. He looked at the others. "You guys hang back about twenty or twenty-five meters. When Archie and I are ready for you to move in, we'll give you the high sign." He nudged Archie. "Lead out, Super Scout."

Archie snapped a salute, then turned and stepped out in a northerly direction. His pace, though slow and careful, was measured and he made good time. Within a half hour, there were dim, dancing lights on the horizon and the noise of the mechanical work on the tanks had grown louder.

Another half hour went by and Falconi ordered a halt.

The patrol, with their M16s locked and loaded, formed up in a skirmish line. Paulo Garcia, the grenade launcher on his weapon loaded with an aerial burst projectile, occupied the center of their combat formation. Gunnar and Blue flanked him as the three worked to maintain the proper distance between themselves and the commander and scout.

If they were discovered at that point, there was no sense in trying to sneak away. They would have to fight their way out of an almost certain-death situation.

Spaced three meters apart, the Black Eagle patrol advanced toward the enemy base. Finally the place came into view. A small generator motor could then be heard among the louder T55 engines. Lights, mounted on tall tripods, illuminated the area, showing the tanks and thatched buildings that made up the garrison.

Falconi, up forward with Archie, was able to speak in a normal tone because of the noisy environment. He pointed to a tank farther out from the others. "That one is ours."

"Gotcha, sir," Archie said. Once again he produced his knife. "I'm ready," he said, slinging his rifle over his shoulder.

Falconi followed the scout's example, drawing his own trench knife—complete with a brass knuckle handle—from the scabbard on his pistol belt.

Blue, Gunnar, and Paulo continued to hang back as Falconi and Archie moved ahead of them. The trio, their rifle muzzles to the front, were ready to react in case things turned hairy and ugly.

Falconi and Archie worked their way toward the chosen tank in a circuitous manner, positioning themselves in a way that they would be out of sight from the other armored vehicles. The entire area was permeated with noise. The soldiers working on the battle wagons added their own bit to the din as they shouted, hammered, and clanged.

Falconi and Archie, lying off in an area of shadows out of the direct light from the bulbs strung around the tank pool, took time to observe the location and circumstances of men and machines.

"Well, Archie, what do you think?"

"What are we waiting for, sir?"

"Let's do it," Falconi said. They moved straight toward the target.

A pair of mechanics had the engine hatch open on the nearest tank. One was making adjustments while the other worked the accelerator linkage, causing the big V12 diesel engine to roar and belch. Falconi glanced at Archie and nodded the signal to move in.

The Black Eagles, the expression on their faces grim and determined, glided forward in this most dangerous and personal form of man-to-man combat—the use of cold, sharp steel.

Archie's target, working the accelerator, was closest. The scout came up behind the man and grabbed him around the neck, pulling him backward. At the same time he deftly slipped the stiletto in under the lower rib, striking upward into the vital organs. The blade cut arteries and muscle, immediately causing massive hemorrhaging.

Falconi's man, suddenly sensing something was wrong, quickly pulled away from the engine and turned around. The lieutenant colonel struck the NVA soldier in the face with the brass knuckles, then cut his throat as he brought the blade back on a follow-through slash. One quick upward stab through the belly, and the mechanic joined his buddy in death.

Falconi looked back at the other three Black Eagles and signaled them forward. They double-timed in. Blue was first, leaping up on the tank and disappearing into the turret. He was quickly followed by Paulo and Archie. Then Gunnar, who would operate the cannon went in next. Falconi, who was going to ride in the tank commander's seat was the last. He settled in, slamming the turret cover down and locking it shut.

Blue, with the engine already running, slipped the big machine into gear and stomped down on the accelerator. The tank treads bit into the dirt, picking up speed surprisingly fast.

"Goddamn it!" Blue suddenly swore. "All these gauges is in Russian. I can't read 'em!"

Falconi, whose mother was a Russian Jew who had escaped Stalin's tyranny back in the 1930's, was fluent in the language. "Not to worry," he said slipping out of his seat. He quickly scanned the dimly lit instruments. "Ah!" he said pointing. "There's the compass. See that letter that sort of looks like a combination 'H' and 'O'?"

"Yes, sir," Blue said.

"That's south," Falconi explained. "So keep that baby lined up." He found another. "*Toldivo,*" he read aloud. "That's fuel. And the needle is on *polni.*"

"Is that good, sir?" Blue asked.

"That means 'full'," Falconi replied.

Blue grinned. "Then it's good."

Falconi returned to his place and found the periscope. He peered through the device, turning it for a rear view. "Nobody's chasing us," he said.

"Not yet, you mean," Archie said from one corner of the cramped quarters.

Gunnar hadn't been wasting his time. He'd fooled around with the 100-millimeter cannon until he figured out how it worked. "Archie!" he yelled over the noise of the engine. "Any artillery ammo down there with you?"

Archie looked around. "Yeah. I've got three racks of the stuff."

"Good," Blue said. "From this point on you'll be my loader."

Archie nodded. The vehicle was hot, noisy, and bouncy as it rolled across the Laotian landscape. "I hate this fucking thing!" he said under his breath.

Paulo didn't say anything. His thoughts were on the North Vietnamese tankers who had burned alive when their battle wagon had been hit by the LAWS.

It seemed a hell of a way to die.

CHAPTER 18

Tim Donegan pressed forward on the throttles making the PBY-5 slip across the waters, gaining speed until its hull broke contact with the waves of the South China Sea.

Choy, checking his maps and notes, said, "Take course of three-five-zero."

"Roger," Donegan replied. Continuing to climb, he eased the big airplane onto the correct heading. "Here we are—three-five-zero."

Chuck Fagin, standing behind the two, glanced out the starboard window at the deep green of the jungle below. "What's our ETA over the Cammon Plateau?" he asked.

Choy again turned his attention to his figures. "We got half-hour flight, Fagin. New idea might work, huh?"

"It better," Fagin said.

They had decided to fill in the holes of their previous search by laying out a pattern that would cover those areas, yet also provide radio cover on parts of territory they'd already searched out. It took Choy's exceptional navigation and map reading skills to lay out the proper azimuths and allow for the important differences between the three norths: grid north, magnetic north, and true north.

All these efforts were necessary in case that Falconi and the Black Eagles were doing lots of moving around and not using any particular place as a base camp.

Clayton Andrews' "liberated" funds had come in handy. Since Fagin's initial purchase of supplies had yet to be delivered to Falconi and his men, the additional monies went strictly to operating the aircraft. If they found the Black Eagles soon enough, there would be extra dollars available for yet another resupply run.

But the pressing problem was to find them.

The chief maintenance sergeant of the tank outfit was a former NCO of the French colonial forces named Tang. His desertion to the communist Viet Minh had been welcomed by the Marxist revolutionaries, but not because of any unique combat experience or leadership ability. Those jungle guerrillas were in sore need of a man with technical expertise when they decided to go to more conventional military tactics and attack the French garrison at Dien Bien Phu.

Now assigned to the armored unit led by the four Russian officers, Tang had quickly learned the mechanical intricacies of the V12 diesel engines under their tutelage. A tireless and demanding worker, he demanded no less from the men serving under him.

On that particular morning, Tang noted that the sun had risen high enough following the night's work that there was no longer a need for the electric lights. He walked over to the generator and flipped the kill switch. The sudden cessation of the engine was scarcely noticeable in the din still created by the crews working on the T55s.

Captain Chin Hoa had ordered that all carburetors be pulled, disassembled, cleaned, reassembled, and reinstalled even if it took twenty-four hours. In addition, the North Vietnamese army officer wanted every engine given a routine tune-up even though they were not due one for several more weeks.

The captain's disenchantment with the Russian advisors had been thinly veiled as he issued his orders. "I do not want the Soviet comrades to find fault with anything," he'd said to Tang. "They have been complaining much lately."

"Yes, Comrade Captain," Tang said. All the men could not help but notice the physical discomfort suffered by the Russians. The tropical weather seemed to wilt the Europeans, making them sickly and lazy. The sudden withdrawal from the mission to find the American unit had not fooled any of the North Vietnamese soldiers. They knew the real reason was that the Russians were ill, not that the carburetors were fouled with dust.

But, because they were Russians, the advisors had to be obeyed with the same enthusiasm and promptness as if they were comrade generals of the North Vietnamese Army. So all engines were being given the unnecessary maintenance treatment as if there really were foreign debris in the works.

Tang began personally inspecting each tank as the mechanics finished up their work. He'd noted one on the far side going out for a trial run. The sergeant was mildly irritated that the crew had not asked permission to do so. Now he was angry because they had not brought it back yet. No doubt the laggards had realized the stupidity and uselessness of the work and had driven off to take a nap. If that was so, they'd find their little escapade had earned them plenty of extra duty.

The mechanics gunned their respective engines for the sergeant's inspection. Each one sounded powerful and tuned as Tang continued his examination of the previous night's work. He kept glancing at the horizon, looking for the erring tank to reappear. If they were late enough that Captain Chin Hoa became upset, then the skylarking maintenance crew would find themselves in a military prison or — worse yet — be sent into the fighting in the Central Highlands as living, breathing mine detectors.

A half-hour later he reached the final vehicle. Before inspecting it, he walked around for another look to see if the missing battle wagon was returning.

Then he saw the two figures sprawled on the ground.

Tang forgot his work and ran over to them. The two mangled corpses, slashed and stabbed, had dried blood caked along with the grease on their uniform. They had been dead for hours. Tang shouted an alarm, then raced back through the tank pool toward the garrison.

His entrance into the officers' quarters was unmilitary, but this disregard for protocol was forgotten when Captain Chin Hoa and the Russian officers noted the expression of alarm on Tang's face.

"Curu toi voi!" Tang shouted. *"Mau len!"* Then,

speaking almost incoherently in Vietnamese, he told the captain what he'd discovered.

Krushenko, sitting at a table enjoying his morning tea and bread, glared over at Chin. "What is he babbling about?"

"Two of the mechanics have been killed," Chin said. "By knife slashes."

"Drunken bastards!" Bulovich, sitting beside Krushenko, exclaimed. "Brawling when they were supposed to be working on tank engines."

Pavlov walked over from where he'd been sitting with Brigis. "You really must improve the discipline in your unit, Comrade Captain Chin."

Chin's jaw tightened perceptively. "The two dead men did not kill each other," he said in a strained voice as he fought his temper. "They were slain during a sneak attack. The tank they were working on is missing."

A moment of stunned silence fell over the Soviets.

"Deserters!" Krushenko finally yelled. *"Proklinat!* Some of your ragamuffins have not only run off, they've taken a Soviet T55 with them!"

Chin scoffed at the idea. "If any of my men decided to desert, they would do so on foot, not drive a tank all over Southeast Asia. Where would they go with it? How could they expect to be unnoticed?"

Now the Latvian Brigis got into the act. "They are probably going to seek out the enemy and turn the vehicle over to them."

"Of course!" Bulovich said. "The Americans would probably pay big rewards for one of our magnificent tanks."

"I don't think so," Brigis said. "Don't they get

plenty every time the Israelis defeat the Arabs?"

"It doesn't matter! We must stop them!" Pavlov shouted.

Chin, now feeling properly chastised, shook his head. "Wait! Let me form up my unit and find out who is missing. Perhaps that will give us a clue as to the destination of the criminals."

"Do so immediately!" Krushenko yelled in a fury. *"Skori!"*

Chin rushed from the building with Tang following. Within a few short minutes the entire North Vietnamese tank company was drawn up on the small parade ground. Like any troops of a totalitarian society, they were used to surprise inspections and headcounts. But the frantic activity accompanying this particular formation confused and alarmed them.

A methodical checking of personnel began with each section leader being required to not only look at his men, but to physically touch each one as an undeniable and certain method of verifying the soldier's presence at the formation.

The end result of the muster was that the only men not present were the two dead mechanics.

Now Chin felt a fresh flush of superiority over the sickly Russians. "My men are all accounted for," he reported with a smug grin.

At that moment, Krushenko felt a stab of cold fear flash through his body. The awful realization of the situation almost made his knees buckle. *"Amerikanski!"*

"What?" Chin asked nervously as he, too, began to figure out what had gone down out there in the tank pool.

175

"Americans, you fool!" Bulovich said. "The gangsters slipped into the camp and have stolen a T55."

Pavlov, the realization of what happened giving him a shot of adrenalin that quickly overrode his physical shakiness, was suddenly ready for action. "What are we to do, *Tovarish Kapitan?*"

"Each of us will take a tank and go after the bastards!" Krushenko said through clenched teeth. He pointed to Chin. "And that includes you. Pick out five of your best crews and have them ready to go."

Chin snapped to attention and saluted. *"Neosredstveno, Tovarish Kapitan!"* he said in Russian. Then he rushed off to obey.

The Russians rushed back to their quarters to begin changing into their combat uniforms. They grabbed their padded tanker helmets and strapped on their personal weapons. Suddenly Krushenko laughed aloud.

"What is so funny, Comrade Captain?" Pavlov asked.

"I am thinking of those poor dumb American bastards," Krushenko answered.

Brigis frowned in puzzlement. "You find something amusing?"

"Of course," Krushenko said. "They are about to go into a tank battle against odds of five-to-one."

Now Pavlov appreciated the situation. "Such a thing in armored warfare is unheard of."

Bulovich laughed. "They do not realize it, but they have committed suicide!"

The name of the UNICEF station was Domo de

Espero.

The words, chosen by the headmistress Uzuri Mwanamke, meant "House of Hope" in Esperanto. She'd chosen this language because of the meaning behind its origin.

Esperanto was not the mother tongue of any particular country. But that doesn't mean it wasn't a real or living language. It had been devised in Czarist Russia in 1887 by Doctor L.L. Zamenhof. It was the oculist's fondest hope that the language become a common denominator between nations and not only ease their ability to communicate with each other, but make their intents and purposes better known and understood on the international level.

Both the name of the institution and the language chosen for it reflected the ideals and aspirations of Uzuri. Raised in Uganda where the soldiery had brutalized civilians on various occasions, this African woman dreamed of a world of peace and harmony where problems and conflicts between nations could be worked out on the diplomatic level. In her own way, by working with the United Nations Childrens Fund—UNESCO—she made a big contribution toward the ideal world.

Uzuri's own exposure to the war in Vietnam began with an assignment to an orphanage. After that she was offered a post as the headmistress of an institution that served not only orphans but also mothers and children who had been displaced by the war. If Uzuri couldn't stop war, she could at least offer comfort and safety to those suffering because of it.

Her staff were mostly locals or residents who were

healthy and intelligent enough to be trained in the rudiments of caring for and feeding a group of psychologically scarred women and children. But, finally, through the efforts of her friend Andrea Thuy, a nurse had been assigned to Domo de Espero.

This was Malpractice McCorkel's wife. On the morning she was due to arrive, Uzuri waited patiently for the arrival. As she worked out the feeding schedules and dispensary appointments for the day, she kept glancing out the window of her office.

Finally, a yellow Volkswagen rolled through the compound gate. It pulled up in front of the administration building and stopped. Andrea and a small, pretty Vietnamese woman got out.

Uzuri rushed from her desk and out onto the small veranda. "Andrea!"

"Uzuri!" Andrea and the other woman walked up. "I would like to introduce Jean McCorkel."

Uzuri offered her hand. "So nice to meet you, Jean."

"I am pleased," Jean said. She had been a civilian nurse at Long Binh medical center, but when she'd learned of the Black Eagles move to Hai-Cat, she'd pulled strings for a job at the United Nations Center.

"Jean, I hope you don't mind starting work this morning without delay," Uzuri said.

"Of course not," Jean replied. "I have already been apprised of the desperate health situation here."

"We do have time for a cup of coffee though," Uzuri said. "I have a fresh pot in my office."

The three women went inside and settled down as Uzuri served the steaming brew. Jean, however, was anxious to at least discuss the situation. "I have brought vaccine with me."

Uzuri clapped her hands in happiness. *"Ahsante Mungu!"* she cried. "We have been facing a smallpox epidemic here."

"Do not fear," Jean said.

Andrea sipped her coffee. "I feel that things will be under control here within a few short days."

"Yes," Uzuri said. She sighed. "I only wish we knew for sure how our men are faring."

Jean set her cup down. "Do you have a man in the war, Uzuri?"

"I have great interest in a man," Uzuri said with a sad smile. "However, I do not think I have the right to think of him as my own."

"Certainly you do," Andrea said.

"But, dear friend Andrea, I do not know if he returns my affection."

"Of course he does," Andrea said. She looked at Jean. "Uzuri is in love with Calvin Culpepper."

"A Black Eagle?" Jean asked. "Then we three women have much in common, don't we?"

"Yes," Andrea said. "We are sisters-in-arms."

"That means we will spend a lot of time together," Jean said.

"Yes," Uzuri remarked. "—praying."

CHAPTER 19

It didn't take Blue Richards long to get the hang of driving the Soviet T55 tank.

Manipulating the steering levers and accelerator, the Navy Seal ran through the gears as he traversed a terrain that consisted of hardpacked flat areas, slight rises, creek beds, and ravines. The big machine performed well, pleasing the driver to no end.

"Yow-eee!" Blue yelled out. "This baby is bad, man! It's bad! I'd just love to make 'shine runs from Dixon Mills to Mobile in this here vehicle. They wouldn't be no revenooers that could tie her down. No, sir! Yow-eee!"

Falconi grinned from his position in the commander's seat. Like the rest of the Black Eagles inside the steel interior, he hung on as best he could as Blue kept the tank close to its maximum speed of 55 kilometers an hour. But, unlike the others who could concentrate all their efforts on enduring the rough ride, the Detachment's commanding officer had to do some quick thinking about the future of the operation they were on.

Naturally, once the T55 was out of fuel, it would be useless for traveling around in. But that would not effect its weaponry. A quick inspection of the interior showed that both machine guns and the cannon were well stocked with plenty of ammo. Although the lack of gasoline would kill its mobile aspect, it could still be used as part of a static defense preparation. A tank was also good for anti-tank purposes. The best thing to do, Falconi decided, would be to locate a good position that offered excellent defenses and dig in with the Russian battle wagon as the centerpiece of resistance. With any luck they could holdout until that damnably late resupply drop reached them.

With that decision firmly established in his head, Falconi turned his attention to the environment of the vehicle. He checked out the periscope first. Then, after nudging the others to follow his example, he slipped on the earphones to check out the intercom.

"Can you read me, Blue?" he asked into the microphone.

"Yes, sir," came back Blue's voice sounding tinny over the Eastern Bloc communications equipment.

"How about it, Gunnar?"

Gunnar nodded. "Yes, sir. You sound kinda funny, but I can hear you alright."

Paulo and Archie were also able to speak to him.

With that fact established, Falconi looked around the turret. A Soviet radio was nestled in a frame to his upper left. He flipped the lever marked *NA* and let it warm up. By turning a switch on the intercom he could hear the hissing of dead air as his commo system locked itself into the wireless device. Now he began slowly rotating the frequency dial, listening to the changing tones of buzzing and whistling. Suddenly absolute silence sounded and the lieutenant colonel knew he'd tuned into some station. Within short seconds he heard a garbled voice saying:

"Falcon, this is Aircraft. Over. Falcon, this is Aircraft. Over."

Desperately searching, Falconi found a handle marked with the Russian word for antenna. He turned it slowly until the voice came in stronger and clearer.

"Falcon, this is Aircraft. Over."

Grinning, Falconi pressed down on the transmit button. "Aircraft, this is Falcon. Where the hell have you been? Over."

The transmission returned with, "Goddamn! Falcon, we been looking all over for you. What's your location? Over."

"You have resupplies? Over."

"Affirmative! Affirmative! And we're ready to drop 'em! Over!"

"Listen to me, Fagin," Falconi said, finally recognizing the voice in spite of the poor reception. "I don't know the coordinates of the Detachment. I'm not with 'em. Over."

"What the hell's going on? Over."

"I'm in a Russian T55 tank heading for the Detachment. Over."

"Falcon, your transmission is garbled or something," Fagin said. "I could swear I read you to say you're in a Russian tank."

"I *am* in a goddamned Russian tank," Falconi said. "If you can find us, we'll lead you over to where you can drop the supplies."

"You are the craziest —" There was a pause then Fagin came back with, "Keep broadcasting and we'll home in on you. Out."

182

Falconi began speaking non-stop into the microphone. He recited the Pledge of Allegiance, the Gettysburg Address, and even sang a few bars of *Rock Around the Clock*. Then he attempted another contact. "Aircraft, this is Falcon. Over."

"This is Aircraft," said Fagin. "We see a Russian tank complete with red star heading due south. Is that you? Over."

"Affirmative," Falconi said. "But let me make a visual check for you. Wait." He opened the turret and stood up looking into the sky. He saw an airplane slowly circling around them. Ducking back down to his seat he once again spoke into the radio. "Aircraft, are you a PBY? Over."

"That's us," Fagin came back.

"Where the hell did you get a PBY?" Falconi asked. He had expected to see a more conventional C130.

"Never mind, pal. Just keep her rolling, pardner. We've got a lot of goodies to get you. Over."

"That's good. But where the hell have you been?" Over."

"It's a long story," Fagin said. "Over."

"All your stories are long," Falconi complained. Suddenly he had an idea. "Can you get us some gasoline? Over."

"Roger that request," Fagin said. "I presume you mean diesel fuel, right? Over."

"Affirmative," Falconi said.

"Wilco. Next run, no sweat. Over."

"That's good news," Falconi said. "Let's go into radio silence. I'll contact you when we're close to the Detachment. Out."

Archie Dobbs, like the others still hooked into the

intercom, could not hear what was going on. All he could see was the commanding officer jabbering away in the microphone. When Falconi finally stopped speaking, Archie stood up and tugged on his trouser leg. "Who the hell have you been talking to, sir?"

"Fagin," Falconi answered. "And he's got the re-supply with him overhead. He'll follow us home, then make the drop."

"At last! Things are looking up, huh, sir?"

Falconi winked. "Super Scout, you've just joined the armored corps."

Sergeant Major Top Gordon walked down the line of Black Eagles manning the defenses that Lieutenant Colonel Falconi had organized along the edge of the mangrove swamp prior to the tank-stealing patrol's departure.

Loco Padilla, standing radio watch, leaned against a durian tree eating slowly out of a can of C-ration peaches. Bravo Team's Prick-Six radio was sitting beside him. The set was turned on with the volume all the way up. The only sound it made was the usual hissing. "Howdy, Sergeant Major."

"How's it going, Loco?"

Loco tapped the can with the plastic spoon. "I'm down to the last can so I'm making 'em last."

Top knelt down and picked up a piece of fruit that had fallen from the tree. "We won't starve as long as the countryside provides edible stuff like this."

"I ain't worried about food," Loco said. He patted the bandoleer beside his M16. "What's got me fretting is the fact I'm running low on bullets and grenades."

"So's ever'body else," Top said. "Too bad there ain't a munitions bush we can pull rounds off of, huh?"

Loco laughed. "Yeah. Or a beer bush, too."

Malpractice McCorkel, not far away, was a bit upset because their conversation had broken into a reverie about his wife Jean. "You two guys are a coupla real dreamers," he said irritably. "You'd both be better off concentrating on the facts of life out here."

"Oh, yeah?" Loco said. "That's what—"

The Prick-Six came to life with Falconi's voice. "Bravo, this is Falcon. Over."

Top didn't wait for Loco to respond. He reached over and grabbed the radio. "This is Bravo. Over."

"I got news, boys," Falconi said. "There's an airplane coming in with resupply. So get the drop zone detail up and moving. Over."

"Wilco," Top happily answered. "Anything else? Over."

"Roger," Falconi said. "I thought you'd be interested in knowing that there is a Russian tank coming in at you. Over."

"Where is the sonofabitch?" Top snarled. "Over."

"Take it easy! Take it easy!" Falconi shouted. "We're in it. I say again. *We're in it!* Do you read me? Over."

"Roger, Falcon," Top said. "We read you five-by-five. Come on in. Out." He jumped up and ran down to the Alpha Team. "Calvin! Get your detail out to receive the resupply! Lieutenant Swift Elk! The old man's patrol is coming back complete with a fucking Russian tank!"

Ray Swift Elk, always the unflappable plains warrior, showed no expression on his copper-colored face. But he said, "Well, now things should start getting interesting around here."

Captain Anatol Krushenko stood up in the turret of his tank. His five-tank command was formed into a "V" formation. He was at the very front while off to his left, slanted back, were the tanks led by Senior Lieutenant Konstantin Bulovich and Lieutenant Dimitri Pavlo. Junior Lieutenant Pavel Brigis and NVA Captain Chin Hoa's vehicles made up the right side of the armored line.

Knowing which direction to go after the stolen tank had been easy. The two tread-tracks left in the yielding soil of the plateau showed up plain enough to be followed in even dull moonlight. In the bright sunshine of day, it was ridiculously effortless and uncomplicated.

All five of the tank commanders sat out in the open, their shoulders and heads above the turret hatch. This was done to ease the ability to see the territory they rode into, although the Russians and their Latvian friend also did so in order to get as much fresh air as possible. But even they forgot the hot weather in the excitement of the chase.

Chin Hoa, on the other hand, had seen a hell of a lot more combat than the Russians had. His time in battle had sharpened his instincts to the point that he did more than simply stare at the tracks they followed. He also glanced around on all sides, noting changes in the terrain while looking for any activity that was either interesting or threatening. His alertness was what made him catch sight of the aircraft. He immediately radioed Krushenko to let him know what he saw.

"Where is it?" the Russian captain demanded.

"Almost straight ahead, Comrade," Chin answered. "It is low on the horizon."

Krushenko got his binoculars and peered through them. Finally he caught sight of the airplane in question. But he could make out no markings on it. He called up the other Europeans.

"It is not a combat aircraft," Pavlov concluded, staring through his own field glasses.

"It is now heading away from us," Bulovich said. "Perhaps it is on a routine reconnaissance mission."

Brigis agreed. "I do not think the Americans we face are from a force large enough to have aircraft assigned to them. This is, as Comrade Senior Lieutenant Bulovich said, a normally scheduled flight over Laos."

"I agree," Krushenko said. "Press on!"

The PBY swept in at under five hundred feet over the area indicated by the panels that Calvin Culpepper had place. Inside the airplane, each standing at an open waist gunner blister, Fagin and Mike McKeever stood poised with air drop bundles.

Choy, squatting in the nose, watched as the markers slid under him. Then he yelled into the microphone, "Now! Now!"

Fagin and McKeever, fighting the prop wash that whipped in through the openings, pushed out the bundles. As soon as the gear dropped free from the aircraft, they each grabbed another and quickly shoved them after the others.

The parachutes blossomed out directly over the panels as the aircraft went into a turn toward the south. A waggle of the wings signaled a farewell, then the PBY climbed for the clouds and the trip home.

Down on the ground, Calvin, Ky Luyen, and Loco Padilla wasted no time in rushing out to grab the deliveries. The parachutes had barely opened, but the three Black Eagles were already beneath them waiting for the supplies to land.

All were experienced when it came to gathering up deliveries. Working as a team, they unhooked the chutes, rolled them up and stuffed them under the bundle straps. When that was done they quickly shouldered the burdens and trotted back toward the swamp as fast as possible under the weight.

They'd no sooner reached cover when the roar of a tank engine sounded just over the horizon. Within moments the T55 hove into view. Falconi, Archie Dobbs, Gunnar Olson, and Paulo Garcia sat on top of the vehicle waving.

Calvin, standing inside the treeline after dropping his bundles, grinned. "Look at that, guys."

"Beautiful, ain't it?" Loco said.

"Yeah, baby," Calvin answered. "We're bad now!"

CHAPTER 20

The Black Eagle Detachment wasted no time in moving the Russian tank into the defensive perimeter. Although there was not enough diesel fuel left to do any aggressive fighting, the next delivery from Fagin would neatly solve that problem.

While everyone watched with great interest, Blue slipped the big machine into reverse. Looking straight out at Top Gordon, who was directing him, the Alabamian slowly backed up, crushing his way through the thick bamboo grove until he reached a point that slightly elevated the cannon tube to give it maximum range.

Top drew his hand across his throat as a signal. Blue cut the engine. "Okay, men," Top said to the spectators. "Let's get to work."

Now the rest of the Detachment began rapidly camouflaging the battle wagon, arranging chopped bamboo around it in a fashion that hid the T55's presence. A vine was even pulled from a nearby tree and wrapped around the cannon to conceal it from view. When that particular part of the project was finished, the tube looked like a large, innocent tree branch projecting outward from the swamp.

The tank also called for some reorganization. Due to Gunnar Olson's skill with heavy weaponry, he was detailed as the cannoneer in the T55. Archie Dobbs was assigned as the loader. His job would be to shove the 100-millimeter ammunition into the breech while Gunnar aimed and fired.

The bundles delivered by the PBY had consisted of three badly needed items: rations, ammunition, and more LAWS. With Gunnar no longer manning one of the anti-tank weapons, Malpractice McCorkel was pressed into duty as a rocketeer. The medic picked up his share of the disposable weapons and carried them down to his fighting position.

Top Gordon passed out ammunition, which included grenades for Paulo Garcia and Loco Padilla. The full bandoleers of M16 rounds were gratefully scooped up by the men from the crates the sergeant major had opened. Steve Matsuno and Malpractice McCorkel were well supplied with conventional ammo in addition to the LAWS.

Everyone got plenty of C-rations, so after the other items had been issued and the defensive plans firmed up, they treated themselves to an orgy of spaghetti and meatballs, beans with franks, crackers, peanut butter, jelly, pound cake, and other goodies.

Archie Dobbs, leaning against the tank, finished off his third can of ham and lima beans. He belched. "Man, it don't get no better than this."

Gunnar Olson, beside him, looked at Super Scout with a shocked expression. "Man, you gotta be kidding! We're stuck all alone out here in a swamp that's smack in the middle of an enemy occupied prairie. We're outnumbered and outgunned and going up against armor."

"Well," Archie hesitantly conceded. "Maybe it can get a *little* better."

Andrea Thuy stood on the dock watching the PBY make a lazy turn for its final approach. The aircraft swayed gently back and forth as its flight path lowered toward the sea. It went onto the surface of the water gently, settling down gracefully between the waves. Finally, with spray flying behind the propellers, it pulled up and rocked to a sudden halt as the pilot Tim Donegan reversed the props and gave the throttles a push.

Mike McKeever made his usual appearance and dropped down to tie up the plane. He did the job quickly, waving over at Andrea. "Hi ya, Toots."

She made a face at him. "Hi, tall, light, and ugly."

McKeever laughed. He knew she didn't like to be called Toots. "We found 'em, Toots."

Andrea immediately forgot her anger. "For sure?"

"We dropped them supplies right in their laps, Toots."

Now Fagin appeared. From the happy way he leaped onto the dock and danced a few steps, it was obvious things had gone all right. "We delivered the goods and are going to get some more with the funds Clayton Andrews brought us," he called out.

"Wonderful! How're they doing?" Andrea asked.

Fagin walked up and slipped his arm around her waist leading her back toward their office. "They're doing great. Can you believe it? They've even got a goddamned Russian tank!"

"How in the world did they manage that?" Andrea asked as they stepped off the dock and walked up through the administration district of Hai-Cat.

"Who knows? I didn't have much of a chance for a chat, but Falconi said to get them some diesel fuel. That's going to be a main item for tomorrow's drop," Fagin said.

"Your news is great and I've got some, too," Andrea said. "It's not as good as yours, but it will be welcomed just the same."

"What's going on?" Fagin asked as they reached their office. He let Andrea precede him, then he followed her in. "Have the Black Eagles been put back on a priority status?"

Andrea went to her desk and picked up a set of orders. "Nothing that good, but some well-deserved promotions have come in," Andrea said.

"For the guys in the detachment?" Fagin asked.

"Not everybody," Andrea said. "But Gunnar Olson is now a staff sergeant, Paulo Garcia is a gunnery sergeant, Blue Richards is a petty officer second class, and Malpractice McCorkel finally made a master sergeant."

"That's great!" Fagin exclaimed. "They've been long overdue. Being in a clandestine outfit like the Black Eagle Detachment doesn't provide for fast promotions."

"I saved the best news for last," Andrea said. "Calvin Culpepper is now a chief warrant officer."

"It's about time," Fagin said. "His technical expertise in engineering and demolitions are enough that he could make a damned good living in civilian life."

"You didn't let me finish," Andrea gently complained. "Ray Swift Elk has been promoted to captain."

"Now there's an All-American success story," Fagin said. "He came in the service as a green buck private off a Sioux Indian reservation. Hell, he didn't even have a high school diploma."

"He certainly took advantage of the opportunities offered by the army," Andrea said. "He's a full-fledged captain now."

"Do me a favor, Andrea," Fagin said. "Fix those papers up for delivery, will you? Word of those promotions ought to go a long way in raising morale. I wonder what caused the brass to decide to give those guys some well-deserved rewards."

"I think Clayton Andrews had a lot to do with it," Andrea said. "I heard he made an appearance in General Taggart's office and really came unglued."

"He's got a lot of clout," Fagin said. "It's not hard to guess what happened after that. Andy probably went clear over Taggart's head and rammed promotions back down the line." Fagin laughed. "The son of a bitch would go clear to the Pentagon if he had to."

"He's a good friend," Andrea said.

"Damn right," Fagin agreed. "Listen up now. I'm going to arrange for a few dozen jerry cans of diesel fuel to drop on the guys tomorrow."

"I'll fix these promotion orders up with a long yellow ribbon tied to them," Andrea said. "That way the guys won't miss them when you toss them out of the airplane."

Fagin laughed and went out to take care of his chore.

Krushenko, flanked by Bulovich and Brigis, lay at the edge of the rise in the ground. All three officers had their binoculars pushed up against their eyes as they looked down at the wide stand of vegetation before them.

"The tracks disappear into that bamboo grove," Krushenko said.

"Da, Tovarish Kapitan," Bulovich agreed. He studied the scene for a few more moments. "That is a swamp. Do you suppose the stolen tank has been mired down in there?"

Brigis, his eyesight momentarily blurring from the concentrated staring, lowered his field glasses. "It is hard to tell. If the marshy area extends very far, I would imagine so. If it is only a patch of mud, the T55 could easily have traversed it and is well on its way farther south."

"They should be low on gasoline by now," Krushenko said. Their own tanks had been supplied with extra jerry cans of fuel before they left.

"Perhaps they have a supply depot," Bulovich suggested.

"Nelepyi!" Krushenko scoffed. "How could they have such a thing? If they were able to logistically support a mechanized effort they would have their own tanks and armored personnel carriers. They would not have to steal one of ours."

"I agree," Brigis said.

Krushenko was a veteran armored force officer. There was nothing in that method of warfare in which he had no experience. That included the proper concealment of vehicles. His expert eyes, assisted by the binoculars, studied each section of the bamboo and durian trees that marked the limits of the mangrove swamp. Suddenly he stopped.

"*Nyu!*" the Russian suddenly exclaimed.

"What do you see, *Tovarish Kapitan?*" Bulovich asked.

"There," Krushenko said. "Just off to the right. Do you see it? It is the tube of a 100-millimeter cannon with a vine around it. At first it appeared to be a thick tree branch to me."

It took the other two several moments before they could spot it. Brigis whistled low. "Excellent camouflaging!"

"Not excellent enough," Krushenko said. "Come. Let us go back to Pavlov and Chin."

The three back-crawled away until they reached lower ground. Then they stood erect to walk back to the tanks. "We have spotted them," Krushenko said.

Chin, anxious for a fight, eagerly asked, "Do we attack them, Comrade Captain?"

"Of course," Krushenko answered. "But not now." He studied the waning light. "It will be dark within a couple of hours. I want plenty of daylight hours to finish them off." He laughed. "They have set up a static defense with the T55. With no fuel they have no other choice."

"It is a good thing you spotted that hidden tank," Bulovich said. "We could have been picked off one-by-one if we didn't know it was there."

"Yes," Krushenko said. "But tomorrow all five of our vehicles will immediately fire on the stolen T55. After we knock it out, we can charge in with machine guns and cannons blazing to finish off the American gangsters."

Bulovich shrugged. "You realize that such a tactic

195

will eliminate any possibility to get prisoners, do you not, *Tovarish Kapitan?*"

Krushenko snarled. "I don't give a damn about capturing them. I want to kill the bastards!"

Chuck Fagin and Mike McKeever wrestled the heavy load of five-gallon jerry cans under the wing of the aircraft that had been positioned over the dock. Choy moved in to help, adding his muscle as they lifted the bundle up to the bomb rack.

"Now!" Fagin yelled out.

Tim Donegan, who had been waiting a couple of paces away, came up and grabbed the top strap. He slipped it into the rack's holding arm and snapped the device shut. "Got it!"

The other three men let loose and stepped back. The other load had already been placed in the opposite rack. The bundles of gasoline were so heavy and cumbersome that Fagin and McKeever would never have been able to wrestle them out of the waist gunner blisters to drop to the Black Eagles. It had been the mechanic's idea to attach them to the bomb racks on the wings. That way, Choy could drop them at the touch of a lever from the bombardier's compartment in the nose.

"It looks like we finished just in time," Fagin said as he noted the tropical night quickly overtaking them.

"It's been a hell of a long day," Donegan said. Like the others he was soaked in perspiration. They had been working since early afternoon in picking up the jerry cans, putting them in a bundle, and attaching the parachutes to them. After that, the

196

heavy burdens had to be lugged down to the dock and finally wrestled up into position to be locked onto the bomb racks.

"Well, boys," Fagin said. "First thing in the morning we take off and drop this to Falconi and his guys."

"Don't forget them promotion orders," Donegan reminded him.

"I didn't," Fagin said. "Andrea fixed 'em up in a package with a yellow streamer. In fact, we'll throw that in on the first pass to test the wind. Then we'll swing back in to drop the fuel to them."

McKeever spat into the oily water around the dock. "Anybody fer a cold 'un?"

"Let's go," Donegan said.

They walked back to the airmen's bungalow. Choy gave Fagin a friendly pat on the shoulder. "I got course all laid out, Fagin. We go straight to Falconi and drop bundle with streamer. I watch it to check wind direction, then we swing back. I guarantee the diesel fuel fall next to tank. It will be just like mama bird when bring food to baby bird."

"They'll appreciate the hell out of that," Fagin said. "They won't have to carry those damned cans too far to fill up the tank."

McKeever laughed. "Yeah! They're gonna pour that stuff into the tank in the tank." He laughed again. "Get it?"

"Yeah," Donegan said. "Real funny."

"I don't see no funny," Choy said.

Fagin tried to explain. "He's using the same word for two different things."

Choy shrugged. "Big deal. Lotsa words like that in Chinese dialects. Not funny."

197

"It won't be funny tomorrow for the Black Eagles if something screws up this operation," Fagin said.

"I don't see no problem," McKeever said.

"Those other T55s undoubtedly must have gone after Falconi," Fagin said. "Those Reds sure as hell won't sit on their asses after one of their battle wagons have been ripped off. If the bastards reach Falconi before us, the Black Eagle Detachment is dead meat."

CHAPTER 21

Calvin Culpepper, sitting on the ground, spread the peanut butter on his last cracker then popped it into his mouth. A couple of moments of chewing followed as he went about the ordeal of swallowing the sticky mess. "Mmmf! This G.I. peanut butter is like wet concrete," he remarked.

Finally, his breakfast finished, he policed up the mess and dropped in the small sump beside him. Then he grabbed his M16 and stood up. "Loco! Ky!" he called out. "Drop zone detail. Let's go."

The two Black Eagles quickly brought their own eating activities to a halt. Dawn was only a few short minutes away. Red shafts of light were already shooting between the trees that bordered the bamboo grove. Loco and Ky joined Calvin and walked out to the edge of the heavy vegetation.

Loco peered eastward. "We can expect 'em anytime, right, Calvin?"

"Yeah," Calvin reported. "I asked for three more guys to give us a hand. Toting jerry cans is hard work."

He'd no sooner spoken than Blue Richards, Paulo Garcia, and Steve Matsuno came out of the bushes. The three men had been sent by Ray Swift Elk to join the work party.

"We hear you guys need a hand," Paulo said. "Is that right?"

"Sure is," Calvin answered.

Grinning, the new arrivals broke into applause. "There you are," Blue said. "We gave you a hand. See you later." He and the other two acted like they were going back to the camp.

"That's real funny," Calvin said laughing. "Just for that I'm gonna make you double-time to the tank with them damn jerry cans."

Now Lieutenant Colonel Robert Falconi made an appearance. "You guys sound like you're having a good time," he said taking a quick gulp of coffee from the canteen cup he carried with him.

"Sure, sir," Calvin said. "Ever'body's in a good mood now that we know they ain't forgotten us."

Falconi started to speak, then he stopped and listened a few moments. Finally he said, "Did you guys hear that?"

"What, sir?" Paulo asked.

"I could swear I heard tanks," Falconi said.

They all listened intently. A slight buzzing noise was soon heard in the distance but it was impossible to identify. Ky pointed. "Look! Airplane!"

A small object could be seen flying toward them. Within a few moments it could be easily recognized as a PBY. "That's what you heard, sir," Blue said. "No doubt. Sound is crazy over this flat country."

"I hope that was it," Falconi said. "Those other

tanks are sure to come rolling in here for a show-down anytime. I want to get those supplies delivered and put to good use before that happens."

"C'mon, Loco," Calvin said. "Give me some help with these panels."

The two rushed out farther into the open and laid out the rectangular-shaped panels in the shape of a "T". The idea was to have the airplane fly down the step toward the crossbar. It was only a few moments later that the big amphibious aircraft rushed over. Chuck Fagin could be seen in the open blister looking down at them. He tossed an object out.

A long yellow streamer unrolled as it streaked toward the ground. It hit a few meters beyond the "T" and bounced. Ky Luyen raced out and grabbed it. He returned and handed it over to Falconi. "A packet with your name on it, sir."

"Thanks," Falconi said. He stuck it under his arm to wait for the plane to turn around and make the run to drop the bundles. He noted that it had gained altitude as it swung out, then came back for the delivery.

"This is it, guys," Calvin said. "We don't want to get caught in the open, so get ready to move fast."

The PBY dropped down, then came straight on. As it passed over the panels it went into a gentle climb. The two bundles under the wings were released and began falling. But instead of coming straight down, they whipped under the aircraft.

The two cargo parachutes deployed, but were so close together they wrapped around each other. The rest of the mishap was that both bundles of jerry cans filled with diesel fuel, spun like two rocks tied together with a string. Whipping around, they

201

streaked groundward toward the tank.

The loads hit directly in front of the T55 exploding and engulfing the vehicle in roaring flames. Immediately the ammunition inside began detonating.

Then a tremendous explosion rocked the tank so hard it bounced up on one side raising the tread off the ground.

Falconi was enraged. "Thanks a lot, Fagin!" he bellowed. "You just bombed our tank, you fucking idiot!"

The sound of the distant explosion caught all the Red tank commander's attention. They stood up in the turrets in time to see an orange and black ball of flame and oily smoke roll up into the sky.

"Did that airplane attack them?" Bulovich asked over his radio.

"Perhaps so," Pavlov answered. "I did not realize we had any air force units in Laos."

Captain Chin Hoa interrupted over his own radio. "I think not, Comrades. The People's Air Force of North Vietnam is concentrating their efforts in the north where the American air strikes are hitting."

The five tank group had noted the airplane's appearance out of the east. Curious, they had watched it sweep in over the enemy positions and drop a long streamer of some sorts. Then it turned around and came back dropping two large objects from its wings.

Then the explosion.

"Push forward!" Krushenko ordered. "Halt when

we reach the elevated ground."

When the T55s reached the position, they ground to a halt. Krushenko, standing up in his seat, studied the objective before them. A good portion of it was in flames. He laughed aloud. "I do not know what happened for sure, but that aircraft could not have done any better for us than if it had been sent in from a Soviet Fighter-Bomber Regiment." He raised an arm as a signal, then spoke enthusiastically into the microphone. "Attack! Attack! Attack!"

The five tankers dropped down into their seats and slammed the turret hatches shut. The drivers gunned the engines and the armored column rolled rapidly forward. The loaders were already cramming high explosive shells into the cannon breeches while the machine gunners began to pick out their preliminary targets.

Andrea Thuy turned her Volkswagen off the main road and drove down the narrow dirt lane that led to Domo de Espero. She went in through the gate and stopped in front of the small administrative building.

Uzuri Mwanamke was already out on the veranda. The Ugandan woman waved and hurried down the steps to the car. She leaned in the passenger window. "You are smiling, *rafiki*. Do you have good news?"

"Yes!" Andrea said getting out. "Let's find Jean so I can tell you both at the same time."

"She is at the dispensary," Uzuri said.

The two, arm-in-arm, walked across the compound to the thatched building. Several women, some holding babies while others tended to toddlers, awaited their turn for medical treatment. They all smiled happy greetings to the two women as they walked past them and into the dispensary.

Jean McCorkel, a stethoscope in her ears, was listening to the heartbeat of an infant. The child's mother, nervously clasping her hands together, watched the nurse work. Jean could only nod to Andrea and Uzuri. She gently turned the child over and monitored its breathing with the instrument. When she finished she spoke soothingly to the mother and went to her medicine cabinet. After filling a small clasp envelope with pills, she explained how to administer the drug. The woman, thanking Jean profusely, picked up her child and left.

"A respiratory infection," Jean explained. "It could be serious back in their home village, but here we can quickly bring it under control."

"I have news," Andrea said. "Good news!"

"The men are safe!" Jean exclaimed.

"Yes," Andrea answered. "And supplies are being delivered to them as fast as possible. But that is not all."

"Who could ask for more?" Uzuri remarked.

"Jean, your husband has been promoted to master sergeant," Andrea said. "And it is about time. If he had stayed in a Special Forces or a regular unit, he would have made the rank three years ago."

"He must be very proud," Jean said. She laughed. "I remember once asking him why the chevrons on his uniform are so faded and old. He explained he had been a sergeant first class for a long, long time."

Andrea grasped Uzuri's arm. "And Calvin is promoted as well. He has been appointed a chief warrant officer."

"I am happy for him, of course," Uzuri said. "Though I must confess to you I have no knowledge of military ranks."

"It is almost like he is an officer," Andrea explained. "He will wear a different uniform and be able to go to the officers' clubs."

Jean, who had a complete familiarity with army protocol, added, "The other soldiers must salute him and call him sir."

"I am sure Calvin will be thrilled," Uzuri said. "I can only hope he will want to share his happiness with me."

"I am sure he will," Andrea assured her.

"At this moment I only pray for his safety," Uzuri said. "Are you sure they are fine?"

"As of this morning, Fagin told me they were healthy and waiting the next resupply delivery," Andrea said. "You realize that is all I can tell you." Security regulations would not permit her to say more.

"May we send messages, Andrea?" Uzuri asked.

"I'm afraid not, dear," Andrea said. "We cannot even let them know they have been transferred to Hai-Cat until they are exfiltrated from the operation they are on."

"That is right," Jean said. "Even my own husband Malpractice does not know we will be able to live together after he returns. It will not be like when they had to stay out at Camp Nui Dep."

Uzuri sighed. "All we can do is wait before we can give them the good news."

"Yes," Andrea said. "I do not wish to dampen the

happy mood, but I suggest we pray for their safe return so that they are able to return to find out the glad tidings."

CHAPTER 22

"Hey!" Archie Dobbs yelled as the exploding Russian tank belched flame and smoke. "My rucksack is in there!"

The fire streaked outward igniting trees and turning stalks of bamboo into charred sticks that looked like burning matches. The concussion swept over the Detachment in an invisible wave, causing them to instinctively blink and duck.

As bits of burning debris and sparks drifted down over the scene, Top Gordon grabbed his poncho and began beating at the spreading blaze sweeping across the outer edges of the swamp. Several more men quickly joined him, trying to keep the fire from destroying all the cover and camouflage they'd arranged there.

"Some of you gather up the ammo and gear!" Falconi bellowed. "Move it back into the swamp. Grab whatever you can on the double!"

Men not occupied in fighting the fire, obeyed quickly, rushing around grabbing ammo, gear, and weapons. They pulled and carried the supplies to safety.

The activities came to a halt when Calvin Culpepper yelled out, "Tanks! Tanks!"

Sergeant Steve Matsuno threw his poncho down and ran back to his other gear. He grabbed three of the LAWS and rushed up to the now bare perimeter. He ignored the smoldering brush, throwing himself down. He took careful aim at the incoming T55. He pressed the trigger boot, sending the rocket swishing across the open space.

The projectile hit the tank turret at an angle, flying straight up into the air before exploding. The armored vehicle turned toward the Japanese-American, its machine guns spitting 12.7 and 7.62-millimeter slugs. The scion of the samurai tradition ignored the splatter of incoming rounds around him as he calmly prepared another LAWS. Once more aiming, he found difficulty in tracking the target that was now weaving back and forth. Suddenly more machine gun bullets flew in, but these were from a different tank.

"Shit!" Steve yelled out pulling back without firing. "Those sons of bitches know what they're doing. They're covering each other instead of separating."

Paulo Garcia, using his M203, sighted in on another T55. He quickly squeezed off the shot, but the M433 armored piercing round didn't live up to its name. It bounced off the apron and detonated harmlessly a few meters above the tank.

"Get the hell back into the swamp!" Falconi ordered. "They'll massacre you out in the open like that."

"Grab the rest of the LAWS and ammo!" Top yelled. "Ever'body get something!"

The Black Eagles instantly obeyed, fading back into the cover offered in the bog while struggling under the load of weaponry and munitions.

Although knee deep in muddy water, they ignored the discomfort as they sought cover behind mahoe trees and among the shrubbery growing out of the fetid wetness of the place.

For a few moments there was calm. But the engines of the battle wagons could be heard drawing closer. Falconi pulled a LAWS off Malpractice Mc-Corkel's shoulder. "Gunnar, get one of those rockets!" he bellowed.

"I already got one, sir!"

"Then go forward with me!" Falconi said. "Steve. Let's go!" The three moved forward, back toward the open space. The five Soviet tanks were in easy view. The Black Eagle commander's battle plan was simple:

"Pick out one and blast it!"

Each man sighted in on a different T55. But before they could fire, the tanks' weapons cut loose, sending automatic fire and cannon shells shrieking toward them. The air ripped with the blast of the incoming rounds. The armored vehicles maneuvered violently but the accuracy of their aim was unaffected.

Three desperately quick firings of the LAWS produced absolutely nothing. Once more an indirect hit was harmless, while two more of the rockets zapped through empty air.

"Haul ass!" Falconi shouted.

The trio of impromptu attackers broke off and splashed back into the heavy vegetation and water. When they rejoined the Detachment, both Top and Ray Swift Elk were waiting for Falconi.

Top was gravely complimentary toward the attackers. "I ain't seen tanks handled that good since I

209

went up against Chinese T34s in Korea."

"They're real pros alright," Falconi said. "And it won't be long before they come crashing in here after us."

Ray Swift Elk looked farther back into the brackish swamp. "We won't be able to go far or fast in there."

"We are at that spot," Falconi said, "that is known as 'being between the rock and the hard place.'"

Tim Donegan took the PBY into a steep bank, turning rapidly back onto the flight line that led to the Black Eagles' position on the ground. "What the hell happened?"

Choy, who had been able to see the bundle drop from the starboard wing, knew exactly what the situation was. "Bundles go under plane. Wrap up and parachute don't open. They turn from resupply to bomb."

Donegan straightened out. "Jesus, look!"

Black, oily smoke bellowed upward as flames licked toward the sky.

Chuck Fagin struggled into the cockpit. "Did you see that? Those damned bundles went out of sight under the fuselage and came out wrapped up together."

"Yes," Choy said. "Bomb racks no good. Design for oblong object with fins. Bundles were hit by propeller wash, sucked into vacuum under plane. Too bad."

"T55s!" Donegan yelled. "And they're attacking Falconi and his guys!"

"Is that .50 caliber still in the nose turret?" Fagin asked.

"You betcha!" Choy replied.

Fagin ducked down and went under the console to the bombardier's position. Grabbing the end of a belt of ammo, he slipped it into the breech of the weapon and slammed the cover shut. After a couple of quick pulls on the cocking handle, he looked through the weapon's sight, lifting the handles until the Russian tanks were in view. Then he fired.

The bullets hit the armor, sparking and ricocheting, but doing absolutely no damage as the PBY streaked past overhead.

Mike McKeever, looking from the port blister, slowly shook his head. He spoke into the intercom. "Them T55s is rolling into the swamp after the Black Eagles."

Choy pressed his face against the window. "The Black Eagles can't go too far in there. They are trapped. Poor Falconi! Poor Black Eagles! *Tsoi-kin!* Good-bye, brave men."

CHAPTER 23

The world seemed to have turned into a blasting, roaring, rocking environment as the hot lead streaking out from the five attacking Russian tanks slapped and smacked around the Black Eagles.

Desperate, but with each individual man trying to think fast, the Detachment pressed farther back into the stinking swamp. Now the water was up to their waists and the mud beneath it dragged and sucked at their boots as they struggled through the murky mire.

Blue Richards, however, was not just blindly splashing around. The Navy Seal went first to Steve Matsuno and dragged the surprised soldier's LAWS off his shoulder.

"What the hell—" Steve sputtered.

"Don't fret," Blue said. Then he sloshed over and did the same to Gunnar Olson. With five of the disposable rockets, he moved quickly to the nearest mango tree. He gauged it to be at least sixty feet high. Slipping the anti-tank weapons across his back, Blue grasped the tree trunk and began to rapidly climb.

Calvin Culpepper, who had been a few meters behind, reached the bottom of the mango at about the time Blue was a quarter of the way up.

"What are you doing, boy?" he yelled.

Blue, gritting his teeth, blurted out, "Them Rooskie tankers cain't see upwards and I'm the best tree climber to ever come outta the state o' Alabama. Now move on before they lay eyes on you and figger out you're jawin' with somebody up this tree! I don't want 'em to know I'm here."

Calvin sloshed on to join the others while Blue continued upward until he reached a forked branch. He shimmied out on it and pulled one of the LAWS free. He could see the closest T55 easily, the hatch to its top turret not more than twenty meters away. Blue aimed, then pumped the firing boot.

The rocket hit true.

Inside, NVA Captain Chin Hoa felt nothing as the blast of mangled steel and shrapnel splattered him and his crew into pieces of gunk that clung to the armored vehicle's interior.

Blue, with showers of leaves falling past him from the backblast, got another rocket. The next tank had now rolled up beside the first. Another careful sight picture, and a second rocket streaked downward onto a hatch cover.

That one ended the military career of Senior Lieutenant Konstantin Bulovich.

The following T55 was at an awkward angle. Blue had to lean out to get a good view of the tank. Hanging precariously, he finally managed to aim. This time the 66-millimeter projectile went into the side of the turret.

Lieutenant Dimitri Pavlov felt the hot blast and had an instant of disorientation as he was smashed against the side of the bulkhead in the battle wagon commander's position. A moment later he realized his tank had been hit and his dizzy mind told him that a fire was imminent. He started to move when he felt his breath sucked out of him. For a blazing millisecond the sensation of burning agony filled his awareness as did the noise of exploding ammunition. Then his flesh was stripped away and his body turned from substance to burned gas.

Up above in the mango tree, Blue had lost his balance. The awkward firing position had caused him to hang out too far over the branch. He clung to the tree as best he could, but when the LAWS around his shoulder slipped off, they pulled him so far that his hands slipped.

Blue fell forty-five feet before he smacked back-first into the dirty water. He went under and instinctively got to his feet, standing up.

The Russian T55, with the tanker sitting up in view in the turret, looked down at him. Captain Anatol Krushenko spoke fluent English. "Now, American, you die!"

Blue knew there was no place to go — except to meet his Maker. Now he felt a surge of what in the south they called *That Old-Time Religion*. "Lord, I ain't got time to say much 'cept I'm sorry for all the bad things I done."

At almost that exact instant, the tank's cannon roared.

CHAPTER 24

Pavel Brigis signaled his driver to bring his tank to a halt as he swung his cannon toward the scene of the action. He saw the American fall from the tall tree and land in the water. The Latvian was surprised when the man, sputtering and spitting, reappeared and stood up in waist deep water.

Then Captain Krushenko's tank rolled up and stopped. The vehicle sent a wave of water cascading out that slapped up against the helpless American. Brigis, who had studied English all his school days, heard Krushenko say, "Now, American, you die!"

Brigis grasped the trigger on the breech and pulled it.

Krushenko's tank took a direct side hit from the Latvian's cannon, blowing up inside with such a roar that dark orange flame — and the Russian's upper torso — shot straight up in the air.

Wasting no time, Brigis pulled his Tokarev pistol from its shoulder holster and dropped down into the interior of his own T55. Three quick shots were deafening in the combined space but the North Vietnamese crewmen who died didn't have time to feel the discomfort. Now Brigis reappeared. He slipped out of the turret and walked down to the sloping hull. The Latvian looked at the American and smiled.

Blue, dirty with muddy water, didn't know what to do but smile back.

"Hello," Brigis said. "How are you? I have a cousin in New Jersey." He tossed his Russian pistol into the swamp water. "I defect."

Blue, taking note of the man's sincerity, continued to smile weakly. "Hang on there, pardner. My skipper oughta be here right quick."

Within five minutes the rest of the Detachment, with Falconi in the lead, returned to investigate the sudden silence in the swamp. When Blue explained what happened, the Black Eagle commander climbed up on the tank. "I am Lieutenant Colonel Falconi of the United States Army."

Brigis saluted. "I am Junior Lieutenant Brigis of the Army of the Soviet Union." He shrugged. "But now I am what I think you call AWOL, no?"

"Yeah," Falconi said. "I need to use your radio."

"Of course," Brigis said. "I will explain it to you."

Ya panyimayu, Falconi said. He slipped inside the tank. Noting the dead crew, he asked, "Did you do this?"

Brigis nodded. "I hardly believe they would approve of my defection to the West. Under those circumstances it seemed that killing them was the best thing to do."

"Yeah. It was probably the *only* thing," Falconi said. "Will there be any more of your former pals showing up?"

Brigis shook his head. "No, Lieutenant Colonel. Without the Russians and myself, the rest of the tank unit is like a snake without a head." He laughed. "They will wiggle back north."

Falconi flipped on the radio and dialed it in. "Aircraft this is Falcon. Over." When Fagin's voice came back, the Black Eagle commander wasted no words. "This mission is completed. Land on the drop zone and pick us up. We ought to be out of this swamp in about fifteen minutes. Over."

"Roger," Fagin said. "How many are we picking up? Over."

"Thirteen," Falconi said. "Over."

"Thirteen? There was only twelve of you who went on this operation," Fagin said. "Over."

"We have a defector. Over."

"Jesus, Falcon, only you could get chased asshole deep into a stinking swamp by five tanks and come out with a defector."

"Hell! There wasn't anything in the OPLAN about *not* getting one, was there?" Falconi asked.

Fagin laughed. "You crazy bastard! Move out to the drop zone. We're coming in. Over."

Falconi smiled. "Wilco. Out."

EPILOGUE

The temperature under the palm trees outside Andrea Thuy's bungalow was quite pleasant. It almost seemed as if it were a spring day back in the Midwest as the three people enjoyed both the shade and the sea breeze.

Lieutenant Colonel Robert Falconi sipped his scotch and soda. "This is the life."

"Yeah," Chuck Fagin said. He was nursing a glass of straight Irish whiskey.

Andrea Thuy laughed. "Why don't you two slugs go down to the beach and join the other guys? They're having a wonderful time."

"Not me," Fagin said. "I went down there just in time to see a big wave knock Archie Dobbs silly while he was trying to bodysurf." He stretched and yawned. "It seemed like such a waste of energy when there's good liquor and cool shade around."

"I agree," Falconi said.

"Wait a minute," Andrea said. "You were down in the surf early this morning."

"I loosened up some," Falconi admitted. "Then I had a little karate workout with Steve Matsuno.

219

Now its time for a lengthy break."

"An intelligent notion," Fagin said.

"By the way," Falconi said. "The guys want me to thank you for going to that extra effort to get supplies to us. Clayton Andrews said you were really humping your ass off."

"Bullshit!" Fagin exclaimed. "If I put out any exertions it was to protect my job."

Falconi gave the CIA case officer a closer look. "I'm beginning to think there's more to you than we've known about."

"There is, Robert," Andrea said.

"Knock it off," Fagin growled.

Falconi shrugged. "Okay." He treated himself to another swallow of his drink. "By the way, what was the full story on that defecting Latvian?"

"Quite an interesting guy," Fagin said, glad the subject had changed. "Like a lot of his countrymen, he hates the Russians. But he played the gung-ho communist role and went into the armed forces working hard for a commission in the Soviet tank corps."

"Really?" Andrea asked. "What was his motive if he wasn't really a dedicated marxist?"

"He wanted to get stationed where an escape across the Iron Curtain would be easier," Fagin explained. "The best chance he had was if he was in an armored unit. He planned on defecting to West Germany, but instead they shipped him to Southeast Asia on a special instruction and training mission. Once he found out that there were Americans in the area, he started working out a scheme to desert. It seemed an impossible dream until they cornered you guys in that swamp."

"We could have really bought the farm," Fagin admitted.

"Especially Blue," Falconi said. "He was looking right down the bore of a T-55 100-millimeter cannon."

Further conversation was interrupted when Andrea's Volkswagen drove up. Chief Warrant Officer Calvin Culpepper and his lady Uzuri Mwanamke got out. They were quickly followed by Master Sergeant and Mrs. Malpractice McCorkel.

Calvin waved. "Let's light up that barbecue!"

"Don't tell me the honeymoon is finally over," Fagin said with a chuckle.

Calvin winked. "It ain't never gonna be over, my man." He slipped his arm around Uzuri's waist as the two couples joined the group.

"It's time to get this party going," Malpractice said.

Jean happily called out, "Hello, Andrea!"

"Where are the others?" Uzuri asked.

"They're down at the beach," Fagin said. "They'll be here pretty quick."

Falconi got up out of his chair. "Well, I'll put the torch to the charcoal."

"I'll fetch the steaks out of the fridge," Andrea said.

Fagin also stood up. "And I'll mix me another drink."

The two marines, Paulo Garcia and Loco Padilla, appeared around the corner of the bungalow. They carried a washtub filled with ice and beer. "It's party time!" Loco crowed. *Viva la fiesta!*

Viva! Fagin called out.

The other Black Eagles began to drift in from the beach as Falconi applied his cigarette lighter to the charcoal. Sounds of beer cans opening and the happy murmur of conversation welled up over the scene. Within short moments, Andrea's record player had been brought out and a new record, Simon and Garfunkel's *Mrs. Robinson*, was soon added to the din of merrymakers.

A feeling of contentment swept over the Black Eagle commander as his men fell into the happy mood for an evening of socializing. For a moment he forgot what part of the world he was in and what his job called on him to do there. The lieutenant colonel tapped his feet in time to the music as the charcoal began to flame.

Then the not too distant sound of the PBY could be heard as it sped along the coast line before lifting into the air carrying Tim Donegan, Choy, and Mike McKeever off on a clandestine CIA mission they'd just received.

The moment of carefree feelings was immediately swept away as the insidious mood of the Southeast Asian War once again swept over Robert Falconi.

Before long he and the others would also be leaving Hai-Cat to carry out another deadly operation in that hell called the Vietnam War.

Archie Dobbs noticed his commanding officer's somber expression. "Hey, lighten up, sir!" he said raising his can of beer. "It's party time!"

Falconi smiled sadly, then turned back to the fire. He raised his eyes toward the horizon.

The PBY was now a small dot, quickly disappearing as it headed north toward bandit country.